"Our child ... ... only be provided by parents who are formally married to each other," Raoul began.

"Accordingly, Molly, I ask you to be my wife. You may rest assured I won't exact the usual privileges of a husband."

Molly stated at Raoul, completely unable to speak. She and their child could enjoy the protection of his name, yet Raoul would be permanently out of her reach.

Your welfare comes first, little one, Molly told her unborn child as she looked up into its father's face. *Being tied to Raoul, yet remaining scrupulously separate from him, won't be easy. But I chose to bring you into this world for reasons that were complex, to say the least. And I owe you the very best possible start in life.*

"All right," Molly said, letting the tension drain out of her shoulders. "I'll marry you if you think that's what we ought to do...."

Dear Reader,

Welcome to Silhouette Romance—experience the magic of the wonderful world where two people fall in love. Meet heroines who will make you cheer for their happiness, and heroes (be they the boys next door or handsome, mysterious strangers) who will win your heart. Silhouette Romances reflect the magic of love—sweeping you away with books that will make you laugh and cry, heartwarming, poignant stories that will move you time and time again.

In the next few months, we're publishing romances by many of your all-time favorite authors such as Diana Palmer, Brittany Young, Annette Broadrick and many others. Your response to these and other authors in Silhouette Romance has served as a touchstone for us, and we're pleased to bring you more books with Silhouette's distinctive medley of charm, wit and—above all—*romance*.

During 1991, we have many special events planned. Don't miss our WRITTEN IN THE STARS series. Each month in 1991, we're proud to present readers with a book that focuses on the hero—and his astrological sign.

I hope you'll enjoy this book and all of the stories to come. Come home to romance—Silhouette Romance—for always!

Sincerely,

Tara Gavin
Senior Editor

SUZANNE CAREY

The Baby Contract

Silhouette *Romance*

Published by Silhouette Books New York

America's Publisher of Contemporary Romance

For Miss Mardo,
with love.

SILHOUETTE BOOKS
300 E. 42nd St., New York, N.Y. 10017

THE BABY CONTRACT

ISBN: 0-373-08777-2

First Silhouette Books printing February 1991

Printed in the U.S.A.

Books by Suzanne Carey

Silhouette Desire

Kiss and Tell #4
Passion's Portrait #69
Mountain Memory #92
Leave Me Never #126
Counterparts #176
Angel in His Arms #206
Confess to Apollo #268
Love Medicine #310
Any Pirate in a Storm #368

Silhouette Intimate Moments

Never Say Goodbye #330

Silhouette Romance

A Most Convenient Marriage #633
Run, Isabella #682
Virgin Territory #736
The Baby Contract #777

SUZANNE CAREY

is a former reporter and magazine editor who prefers to write romance novels because they add to the sum total of love in the world.

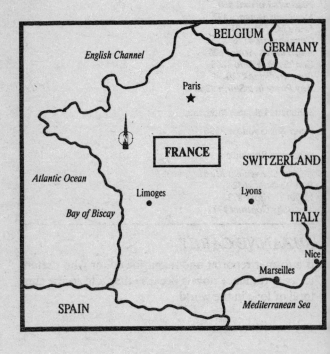

Prologue

Plonk. Plonk. Ker-thunk. The hollow sounds made by Moira Kathleen Fitzwilliam's bare feet as they struck the diving board reverberated in the bright Minnesota afternoon. Bouncing, she sprang free and sliced through the air in an almost perfect one-and-a-half gainer. Her twelve-year-old body, thin and angular except for the budding swell of her breasts, broke the water with arrowlike precision and sped toward the bottom of the pool.

I nearly had it! she exulted, invading sun-spangled depths. By the time school opens, I will. Mr. McNair won't believe how good I am.

Applause from her mother and Aunt Rosie greeted her as she surfaced, pushing wet strands of dark hair out of her eyes.

"Great job, Molly!" her mother called. "Did you see that, Joe?"

"I sure did," her father confirmed, glancing up from his *Wall Street Journal*. "Keep it up, baby. You're a cinch to make the team."

Leaning into a lazy sidestroke, Molly swam over to the side of the pool. As she grasped the concrete apron with one hand, a silvery peal of laughter floated across the lawn. Heads turned in anticipation. Siobhan! Molly thought with a little shiver of excitement. The very air seemed to scintillate with possibilities whenever her older sister was around.

"They're here!" Kathleen Fitzwilliam exclaimed, jumping delightedly to her feet. "Oh, Rosie...can you believe it? My little girl is twenty-four and soon to be a wife!"

"The sooner, the better if you ask me," Joe grumbled, setting his paper aside. "This is starting to cost me a fortune." But he was smiling, too.

Molly watched as Siobhan hugged her parents and Aunt Rosie, and introduced them to her fiancé. Though Joe and Kathleen Fitzwilliam had flown to Paris to meet Raoul de Montfort when he and Siobhan had announced their engagement, Molly and her mother's sister, Rosie O'Meara, who had come to Duluth from Florida for the wedding, had been forced to make do with photographs.

Instead of the newcomer, Molly's laughing, teasing sister rapidly became the center of attention. Molly often thought of her as a swan who had emerged by happenstance in a family of moderately good-looking ducklings. Arranged in a mass of curls, Siobhan's auburn hair framed her face like a halo. Her figure was willowy, her green eyes sparkled, her smallest gesture was the essence of verve and grace. According to Aunt Rosie, who was a late-night movie buff, Siobhan had the luminous glow of a Katharine Hepburn combined with the sultry allure of a Rita Hayworth. The result had drawn a host of male admirers since she was in the seventh grade.

For once, however, Molly didn't continue to look adoringly at her sister and wonder how such a magical creature could be related to her. Out of curiosity she focused on the man Siobhan had agreed to marry. The scion of a wealthy French family, twenty-seven-year-old Raoul would inherit a title someday. He was tall and lean with the kind of compact build that hinted at hard muscles beneath his raw silk jacket and stylishly pleated trousers.

His pictures don't do him justice, Molly thought, gazing at emphatic brows and thick, dark hair that looked as if you could smooth it down beneath your hand like the pelt of a healthy animal. Briefly he turned his head and she noted a firm, aquiline profile. Though he had a wry smile that made laugh lines deepen beside his mouth, there was something pensive about his eyes.

About to get out of the pool, Molly hesitated. I probably look like a drowned rat, she thought, suddenly self-conscious about her appearance. I wouldn't want him to get the wrong impression.

A moment later Siobhan was catching him by the hand and leading him in Molly's direction. "I want you to meet my sister, Molly," she said.

Looking down at Molly, Raoul didn't speak for a moment. She was just a skinny, dark-haired kid. Yet there was something special about her that tugged at the heart. As she looked up at him, her brown eyes glowed with some kind of discovery. Her long, wet lashes stuck together like the points of stars.

"You didn't tell me your sister was a changeling, a gypsy princess, *chérie*," he murmured at last, hoping neither she nor Siobhan would think he had lost his mind.

"Did you notice?" Molly asked Aunt Rosie as they were getting dressed for the rehearsal dinner. "Though his eyes are hazel, they have the most beautiful golden rims around the irises."

Apparently she didn't have to name the person she was speaking about.

"I couldn't vouch for that," Aunt Rosie answered, chattering as usual to Molly as if she were an adult. "But I have to hand it to Siobhan. He's a real prize—smart, good-looking and manners like a prince. If he weren't 'old money' and in line to be a count someday, he could always make ends meet as a movie star."

Applying natural lip gloss with an inexpert hand, Molly wholeheartedly agreed. As wonderful as she is, Siobhan's very lucky to have him, she thought. Imagine getting married to someone who looks and talks that way. For the first time, she began to realize what the attraction between men and women was all about.

Downstairs, more people were arriving, including the best man, a Frenchman of Russian extraction who had attended the Sorbonne with the groom. Unfortunately none of Raoul's family members had been able to make it. Count Henri, his father, was in ill health.

When she and Aunt Rosie walked into the living room, Molly was glad she'd allowed her mother to choose several new outfits for her. The white silk organza party dress with short puffed sleeves that could be worn off the shoulder might not have been as comfortable as her favorite jeans, but it made her feel grown-up, even a little glamorous. Talking her father into letting her have half a glass of wine, she perched on the back of a couch and watched Raoul move among the other guests until it was time to leave for the church.

As a junior bridesmaid, Molly had to practice walking down the aisle until she got it right. Meanwhile, Molly's brothers, Matt and Sean, were drilling for their assignment as ushers. Pronouncing herself bored with the whole proceedings, Siobhan excused herself to powder her nose. When she was needed to go through the actual motions of the wedding ceremony, they couldn't find her anywhere.

"I'll get her," Molly offered, darting out of the nave's side entrance before her mother could protest.

She guessed her sister had disappeared to have a cigarette. Neither her mother nor her father knew Siobhan smoked, and Raoul probably didn't, either, thanks to her judicious use of breath mints. Bet I know where she is, Molly thought. Out behind the sacristy, in that little grove of trees.

Siobhan didn't hear her light footsteps. To Molly's distress, the reason for that sensory lapse immediately became apparent. About to be wed to the kind of man other girls only dreamed about, her big sister was locked in the embrace of a boyfriend from college days.

"What...what do you think you're doing?" Molly choked.

Guiltily the two figures moved apart. Siobhan's green eyes registered panic, but only for a moment. "Oh, it's you, Molly," she said, sighing with relief. "You remember Dan, don't you? He dropped by to say hello. We were just exchanging a hug for old times' sake."

"Umm, yes. Hi."

But though she didn't say anything more in Dan's presence, Molly was far from convinced of Siobhan's innocence. In truth, she felt shocked at her sister's conduct. Didn't Siobhan love Raoul?

"How could you do a thing like that?" she asked worriedly as they returned to the rehearsal.

Siobhan shrugged her elegant shoulders. "Like what?"

"Kissing Dan Rainey on the lips."

About to enter the church, Siobhan drew Molly aside. "Let me explain something to you, little sister," she said as if imparting a pearl of wisdom she expected Molly to treasure. "Raoul is special. But the world is full of beautiful men."

Siobhan's wedding day was made-to-order. From her bedroom window, Molly looked out at dappled sunlight filtering through the trees, the white sails of a regatta on Lake Superior. There wasn't a cloud in the sky.

In her bridal gown and headpiece, which were hand-decorated with thousands of tiny iridescent pailettes, Siobhan was like a vision out of a fairy tale. Already dressed in the pale blue formal creation she would wear, Molly caught her breath as she gazed through the open doorway of her sister's room. "Oh, Siobhan," she whispered. "You're absolutely ravishing."

To her amazement, the bride-to-be was anything but pleased by the remark. "I *hate* this headpiece," she fussed at her mother and Aunt Rosie, pausing to grimace at herself in a full-length mirror. "I should have chosen the other one. Now it's too late."

Uneasy at her sister's mood and still puzzled over Siobhan's comment of the night before, Molly ran downstairs to find Matt. At twenty-five, freckled, red-headed Matt was studying for the priesthood. Unlike her parents he could be counted on to give thoughtful, adult answers to all her questions.

She found Matt having coffee at the kitchen table. Together they strolled to the summerhouse, keeping to the path so Molly's dress wouldn't get grass stains on the hem. After extracting his promise that he wouldn't pass along the tale to anyone, she described the scene she'd stumbled across the night before and repeated Siobhan's explanation.

"What did she mean, 'Raoul is special. But the world is full of beautiful men?'" Molly asked.

A disapproving frown drew Matt's sandy brows together, and he didn't answer for a moment. "Marriage is a serious commitment," he explained at last. "People can get all worked up, thinking about spending the rest of their life with a particular person. That's why there are bachelor and bachelorette parties... to let off a little of that steam. I trust that's what Siobhan was up to last night."

Despite her early-morning jitters, Siobhan's wedding was perfect in every detail. She pledged her troth to Raoul in a strong, clear voice with every appearance of stars in her eyes. Kathleen Fitzwilliam and Rosie O'Meara were wiping away tears.

As she watched the nuptial kiss from her place among the bridesmaids, Molly had a peculiar ache in her throat. How must it feel, she wondered, to be crushed in Raoul's strong arms that way? She hadn't liked it when Tim Connally had cornered her outside the school lunchroom and pressed his lips against hers. But Raoul was different. For some reason, the thought of being kissed by him filled her with guilty excitement.

Her parents were close friends of the Bishop of Duluth, and the High Mass he celebrated to honor the union of Siobhan Rose Fitzwilliam and Raoul Beaulieu de

Montfort seemed to go on forever. Afterward, the newly wedded pair stood outside in the sunlight, hugging and kissing everyone. Not certain what motivated her restraint, Molly threw her arms around Siobhan but limited her congratulations to Raoul to a solemn handshake.

The wedding breakfast passed in a blur. Next came photographs and then it was time to return to the white-pillared Northland Country Club for the reception. Asserting that Siobhan would only marry once, Joe Fitzwilliam had hired a six-piece orchestra. Champagne was flowing freely and the cake had already been cut by the time Raoul asked Molly to dance.

"I...I don't know how," she stammered, avoiding his eyes.

"Ah, but my wife tells me otherwise," he insisted, grasping the fingers of her right hand and placing his other hand on her waist. "She says your parents have paid for some very expensive lessons. Why not put them to good use?"

Just to have Raoul touch her sent goose bumps of fright and anticipation racing over Molly's skin. But it was useless to protest. They were already dancing, to the indulgent smiles of her parents and some of the other guests. Imprisoned lightly in her new brother-in-law's arms, she was dizzy with the scent and feel of him, half-incoherent at the strong vibrations of his male allure.

Though it wasn't the well-bred thing to do, Molly sighed audibly at the number's end. But to her dismay, Raoul had saved the ultimate imposition for last.

"Outside the church this morning, you cheated me of my due," he reminded softly. "Each of the bridesmaids must kiss the groom."

Before she could stop him, he leaned down and feathered a chaste, utterly gentle kiss on her mouth. The effect was so startling Molly found herself incapable of breath. She felt as if the earth had stumbled on its axis, throwing every comfortable precept of her existence in doubt.

She wandered through the rest of the reception in a daze. Like a sleepwalker, she danced with Theo Spassky, Raoul's best man, and several boys close to her own age. When everyone returned to the Fitzwilliams' London Road home and Siobhan tossed her bouquet from its curving staircase, Molly was startled to find the arrangement of orange blossoms and stephanotis clutched tightly in her fingers.

What's the matter with me? she thought, distractedly inhaling its perfume. I've never acted like this before. It was only as the bride and groom drove off in the sleek gray limousine Joe Fitzwilliam had rented for the occasion that she realized the awful truth. At the age of twelve and completely lacking in experience with men, she had fallen head over heels in love with her sister's husband.

Chapter One

If it hadn't been for Raoul de Montfort, Molly thought, noticing the dark-haired young girl who had come into the shop with her mother, I wouldn't have married Kirk Dunlap. He wouldn't have cheated on me and we wouldn't have had that terrible argument. Maybe...just maybe...he wouldn't have crashed his jet on a training mission outside Homestead Air Force Base last spring. And I wouldn't be a widow at twenty-three.

She'd been trying to prove something by marrying the dashing young pilot who claimed to worship the ground she walked on, Molly knew. In essence, she'd been attempting to exorcise a ghost. But it hadn't worked, any more than it had sufficed to remain a stranger to her sister's Paris residence over the years. The image of Raoul—wry, handsome and brooding, with a propensity for doing or saying the unexpected—was always there in the back of her head.

Or maybe it was the back of her heart.

The girl in the shop reminded Molly of the self she'd been at Siobhan's wedding: thin, gangly but athletic, still lost in the dreamworld of adolescence. But perhaps she was a year or two older. That would make her fourteen or thereabouts, Molly thought. The age I was when my parents died.

Both the girl and her mother were newcomers to Rosie O'Meara's exclusive blue-and-white awninged Palm Beach boutique. Probably they were tourists.

"May I help you?" Molly asked them with a smile.

For some reason, the customers who seemed most intimidated by the Via Mizner's upper-crust ambiance found her manner particularly reassuring.

"Yes, please," the mother said. "We're somewhat unfamiliar with the shops in this area. I'm looking for a dinner dress.... Something cool and tropical."

Without seeming to do so, Molly studied the woman's hair and skin color. She had already estimated her size and likely budget constraints.

"I think we may have the very thing," she murmured, leading her to a rack of specially priced frocks.

Molly's mother, father and brother Sean had been killed in a head-on car crash in Minneapolis two months after her fourteenth birthday. Her hands riffling through silk and linen designer creations as she sought what she was looking for, she remembered screaming in disbelief when Matt had broken the news.

With the deaths of the senior Fitzwilliams, the secure, familiar world of Molly's childhood had collapsed overnight. What would happen to her, everyone had whispered? Perhaps she should go to Siobhan in France. She certainly couldn't expect to live with Matt in the rectory to which he'd been assigned.

Ultimately, despite her tender age, Molly had made the decision herself. Living with Siobhan and Raoul had been out of the question. Instead she'd come to Florida and taken up residence in Rosie's breezy, elegant mansion on the Intracoastal Waterway. Gradually the tragedy of her parents' deaths had receded, and the big Mediterranean-style stucco house had become a second home.

Under her widowed aunt's guidance, the awkward but promising duckling Raoul had kissed at Siobhan's wedding had metamorphosed into a swan of sorts. She'd graduated from high school with honors and her share of beaux, earned a degree in fashion merchandising in Atlanta and had come home to begin working toward a partnership in the boutique. Money hadn't been a problem. Her parents had left her a generous trust.

Then Kirk Dunlap had come along and something about him—his dark good looks or extravagant way with words, perhaps—had reminded her of Raoul. She had let him sweep her off her feet. Yet not once in the eight months she'd spent as his wife, living in base housing and enduring the brusque, groping intimacies of their marriage bed, had she experienced the heady anticipation and tremulous delight Raoul had so effortlessly evoked.

I guess I've seen my sister's husband a total of four times in the past eleven years, she thought as she ushered her customer into a posh dressing room. Once at his wedding and again at Matt's ordination. A third time at my parents' and Sean's funeral. Raoul had been too busy with his political career as a deputy in the French National Assembly to fly back to the States when she'd gotten married or when Kirk had died.

That left her brief visit to Paris the summer she was seventeen. She and Rosie had been touring the continent as a kind of advance high school graduation present and, though Molly would have preferred it otherwise, they hadn't been able to come up with a legitimate excuse for not staying with the de Montforts. There had been something very gratifying about the admiration in Raoul's eyes as he'd taken in Molly's lithe, grown-up figure and hesitant smile even if it made her nervous to respond to him that way.

Yet though she'd found him as wonderful as ever, she'd been worried by the changes she'd seen in him and particularly in his relationship with her sister. Always difficult to read and admittedly preoccupied with French politics, Raoul had become closed and distant. Meanwhile Siobhan had embraced the role of social butterfly. Surrounded by a coterie of moneyed and indolent friends, she had flitted restlessly from party to dance club, couturier fitting to gallery opening. No children had come along to bless their union or cramp her style. There had seemed to be nothing of substance to draw them together.

To Molly's satisfaction, a rose-colored linen dress with matching fluted jacket by one of the newer designers enhanced her customer's less-than-perfect figure and brought out her lovely complexion. It always pleased her to see the transformation that took place in a woman's eyes when she tried on an ensemble that was destined to become one of her all-time favorites.

"That outfit looks smashing on you," she said, her obvious sincerity softening the hackneyed words.

"It really does, doesn't it?" The girl's mother turned this way and that, admiring herself in the three-way mirror. "What do you think, Susie?"

"Pretty nifty, Mom." The dark-haired teenager gave her mother a benevolent look. "Dad's going to fall for you all over again," she said.

"Then I absolutely must have it. Even if it's more than I was prepared to spend." The woman turned to Molly. "I do hope you take credit cards."

Aunt Rosie relieved Molly in the shop at about four. "I'm so glad Matt's coming to dinner tonight," she remarked as her niece gathered up her things. "Though he's assigned to a parish in Ft. Lauderdale, we don't get to see him as often as I'd like."

Driving home to the big house on Lake Worth, Molly thought how fortunate it was that Matt's superiors had allowed him to transfer to Florida after Joe and Kathleen Fitzwilliam died. In a way, he and Aunt Rosie had become substitute parents to her. She wasn't sure how she would have managed without them.

The telegram was lying on the hall table when she walked in, her heels clicking against the cool Cuban tiles. "It's for you, Miss Molly," her aunt's housekeeper announced, wiping her hands on her apron. "I had to sign for it. I hope that was all right."

"Of course, Caroline."

Curious, Molly ripped open the envelope and scanned the message it contained. The telegram was from Siobhan. *Need your help,* her older sister announced. *Will phone tonight.*

Siobhan, asking for her help?

I wonder what this is all about, Molly thought, popping into the kitchen to check on preparations for their evening meal before running upstairs to shower and change. I can't imagine the sort of emergency that would prompt Siobhan to call on me. She's always been closer to Matt, probably because of their proximity in age. To her, I've always been a kid, the family afterthought.

Stripping off her clothes in her peaches-and-cream boudoir, Molly asked herself why Siobhan hadn't turned to Raoul. With such a husband, why would she ask her younger sister for help and consolation?

Maybe Raoul's the *problem*, she speculated suddenly, letting the lukewarm spray of the shower flow like a caress over her skin. I'm not the only one in the family who has a strong suspicion they haven't been getting along. But I can't believe he's asked her for a divorce. The de Montforts are as dead set on the indestructibility of marriage as the Fitzwilliams have always been.

What, then? she asked herself, squeezing some bath gel onto a sponge. Is he having an affair? Or seeing several women on the side? Given Siobhan's propensity to flirt with everything in trousers, she didn't find that possibility too difficult to believe though she deplored it. If he *is* involved with someone, Molly thought, I don't know what she expects me to do about it. I didn't even have what it took to command my own husband's loyalty though we were still newlyweds.

Resolutely she pushed the pain of Kirk's perfidy aside. That was in the past and best forgotten. She didn't plan to marry again.

Take it easy, she cautioned herself, returning to the subject at hand. You're blowing this way out of proportion. Siobhan just wants you to conduct some business for her stateside—something private she and Raoul don't want the rest of the de Montforts to know about.

It struck her that Siobhan might have a medical problem. Instinctively she realized that, in such a situation, her older sister would want to keep things to herself until a diagnosis had been made. But Molly couldn't imagine her vibrant sibling suffering from any kind of illness. Stubbornly her instincts insisted her sister's problem was somehow related to Raoul.

Drying off with a luxuriously thick terry towel, she sat at her French Provincial dressing table to brush her hair and reapply her makeup. The slender, dark-haired young woman who gazed back at her from the oval mirror looked nothing like Siobhan, let alone Rita Hayworth or Katharine Hepburn. I'm more the Jean Simmons type, she acknowledged. Gamin and wholesome. She had her own kind of elegance. Yet she wasn't displeased by the notion. There was something calm in her wide brown eyes that hadn't been there before her young husband's infidelity and untimely death. It stated quietly but firmly that here was someone who knew her own mind but didn't have unrealistic expectations. If life gave her lemons, she would make lemonade.

Arriving home at about six, Aunt Rosie changed into one of her exotic silk caftans and mixed an ice-cold pitcher of very dry martinis. A creature of habit, she carried the pitcher out onto the breeze-cooled loggia along with a bowl of salted mixed nuts. Matt was crazy about munchies but he didn't often get them at the rectory where he lived. He arrived soon after, thin and slightly balding at thirty-six, in a somber black suit. He wore the usual stiff Roman collar. Yet there was still something boyish about him. He had the same spattering of freckles, the same wide, approving smile Molly remembered from his youth.

"How are my two best girls?" he asked, giving them each a fond hug. "As busy and prosperous as ever, I trust?"

Plopping an extra olive into his drink, Aunt Rosie waved Matt to a chair. "Since I made Molly a full part-

ner, *Rosie O'Meara's* has been outrageously successful," she said. "We had the best winter quarter of anyone
on the beach. In case you didn't know it, your baby sister is quite an accomplished businesswoman."

"I never doubted it for a moment."

Molly flushed at the praise. Yet she knew Aunt Rosie
wasn't exaggerating. With her marketing and display
skills, she'd helped lift the boutique into a category of its
own among the area's unique and exclusive shops. Her
commitment to its success had brought her a great deal
of satisfaction, easing the grief and loneliness in her
heart. Because of the shop, she'd become a woman with
a purpose. Only her romantic, domestic side seemed
destined to go unfulfilled.

"I got a telegram from Siobhan this afternoon," she
remarked, shifting the focus of the conversation away
from herself.

Both Matt and Aunt Rosie looked at her in surprise.
"Is anything wrong?" Matt asked.

Molly shrugged. "I'm not sure. She said she needed
my help. But she didn't elaborate. She promised to call
this evening. You can ask her yourselves."

Aunt Rosie shook her head in disbelief. "It's not like
Siobhan to ask for assistance from anyone," she said.
"Least of all, you, Molly. No offense. But you know it's
true. She doesn't realize what a capable young woman
you've become."

Matt seemed to find the telegram somewhat strange, as
well. He swirled his drink with a thoughtful, faintly
worried expression.

"Whatever Sib's problem is, I have a feeling it's been
developing for quite some time," he said at last. "Ever
since I can remember, she's pursued superficial plea-
sures in lieu of more lasting contentment. As for

Raoul . . . well, I hardly know him. But he seems fairly dissatisfied with their situation. The last time I saw them together, I formed the strong impression of a man who was holding his tongue with great difficulty. I wonder if there's been a falling-out between them.''

As usual, Molly felt uneasy when Siobhan's relationship with her husband was being discussed. Though she'd never acted on it, her attraction to Raoul had only deepened. God knows why, she thought as they went into the dining room to partake of Caroline's superb capon with oyster dressing. I've done everything I could to root it out—making myself scarce, refusing to daydream about him, even marrying another man.

Yet just a hint that his union with Siobhan might be in trouble sent ripples of excitement coursing through her most lawless self. If her older sister and Raoul broke up, that self argued, there might be a chance for her. Bitterly ashamed of such thoughts, Molly vowed to do whatever she could to help Siobhan straighten out her marital problems.

They were just finishing dessert when Aunt Rosie's housekeeper announced her sister's call.

''Please bring the portable phone in here, Caroline,'' Molly requested with a little frisson of anticipation.

A moment later, Siobhan's husky, effervescent tones sped over the satellite connection. ''Molly, darling!'' she exclaimed. ''Is that really you? Did you get my telegram?''

''Yes, it's me.'' Overwhelmed by Siobhan's high-voltage personality, Molly retreated to matter-of-fact seriousness. ''And yes, I got your message. It was waiting for me this afternoon when I got home from work.''

''Then you realize I want you to do something for me.''

Try though she would, Molly couldn't detect a trace of anxiety or stress in her sister's voice. "Yes," she answered. "I've been rather curious about what it is."

A pause followed. It didn't last long. But Molly could feel the wheels turning in her sister's head.

"'Fraid I can't tell you now . . . not over the phone," Siobhan acknowledged at last. "The walls have ears. I want you to come to Paris so I can explain everything in person. Naturally I'll be happy to pay your fare. I'll have the airline issue you a ticket just as soon as you give me a departure date."

Molly was dumbfounded. "I . . . I don't know what to say," she stammered after a moment.

"Simply say *yes!*"

As usual, Siobhan blithely assumed she could count on Molly's cooperation. A few details remained to be worked out, that was all. Whatever scheme she was planning would go forward without a hitch.

Again Molly didn't answer immediately and the line hummed empty between them. Was Siobhan really so anxious to see her that she'd volunteer the price of passage, she asked herself? Or was she merely imagining things? What possible service or comfort could Molly provide that would place her in such high demand?

The walls have ears, her sister had warned. Molly's notion that she was in some kind of trouble only deepened, despite the easy assurance that rang in Siobhan's voice.

"Give me a minute to think," she proposed hastily. "Matt and Aunt Rosie are here tonight. Why don't I let you talk with them for a moment?"

As she was well aware, her own responses had been as cryptic as her sister's from a listener's point of view. Eagerly Matt grabbed the phone. In his quiet but forceful way, he demanded to know just what Siobhan's telegram was all about. From the look on his face, he didn't get any further than Molly had.

"Yes, yes... I know it was *Molly* you contacted," he acknowledged in a frustrated tone. "But we all care about your welfare...."

A moment later, with an exasperated, "Have it your own way, then," he passed the receiver to his aunt.

From what Molly could gather, Rosie O'Meara's tactful fishing expedition was similarly without result. Meanwhile her own brain was doing somersaults. Think! she ordered herself sharply. This transatlantic call is costing your sister some money. It's only fair you give her an answer.

Just a short time earlier, burdened with guilt over her feelings for Raoul, she'd promised herself she would help Siobhan in any way she could. Now, confronted with a request to visit the de Montforts in Paris, she found herself wavering. If she went, she'd have to see Raoul on a daily basis, live temporarily under his roof. Perhaps even take Siobhan's part against him in a family argument. Much as she loved her sister, she would find that very difficult.

But maybe it didn't have to be that way. The Raoul you fell in love with so long ago doesn't exist anymore, she reminded herself. People change over time. And you never really knew him anyway. This may be the very chance you need to lay a childish passion to rest.

With a puzzled, semiprovoked expression that was a twin to Matt's, Molly's aunt handed her the phone.

"Well?" Siobhan demanded, going straight to the point as she always did. "Can I count on your help?"

Given her status as a woman of independent means and a full partner in the boutique, it was well within

Molly's power to grant her sister's wish without stopping to consult with anyone. Yet instinctively she hesitated.

"I can't give you a definite answer tonight," she said at last. "I have responsibilities, you know.... The shop, for one thing. I was planning a buying trip to New York next month. But I'll do my best to work things out. I'll have to let you know in a few days."

"Hold on a second." Apparently muffling the receiver, Siobhan spoke to someone at her end. Then, "It's Molly," she acknowledged more clearly. "Would you like to speak with her?"

A moment later, Raoul's raspy, French-accented voice came over the line. "*Allô,* Molly," he said. "It was good of you to call. How are things in Florida?"

Seated at the dining room table with her brother and her aunt, Molly felt the old familiar tremor of excitement feather over her skin. The six years since she'd seen him and the more than five thousand miles that separated them notwithstanding, Siobhan's husband could still evoke the most vulnerable aspects of her womanhood.

"Hot," she said as casually as she could. "And humid. The shop is practically running itself."

"*Eh bien....* Why don't you come and see us?"

Something about the way Raoul put the question made Molly realize Siobhan hadn't consulted him before issuing her invitation. There was also the odd fact that Raoul thought *she* had called. Why all the subterfuge?

"Maybe I will," she responded shyly.

Despite her best intentions, the genuine pleasure of his reaction touched her heart. "Please do," he encouraged. "Paris is particularly lovely in the spring."

Molly breathed an inaudible sigh of relief when Siobhan came back on to say *au revoir*. But she had a pretty good idea what she'd be dreaming about that night.

"Would she tell *you* what she wanted?" Matt asked with a slight edge in his voice as she hung up the phone.

"Not really." Guiltily hugging the memory of Raoul's warmth to herself even as she repudiated the thought of anything happening between them, Molly wasn't ready to discuss the various possibilities that had occurred to her. "She said she couldn't tell me very much over the phone. Apparently whatever her problem is, she doesn't want the rest of the de Montforts to know."

They had to be satisfied with that. Returning to the loggia with them to watch the sunset, Molly listened as her brother and aunt spent the rest of the evening in fruitless speculation. No matter how many theories they evolved, the motive behind Siobhan's extraordinary request remained a giant question mark.

Only time and a journey to France would provide an answer. Meanwhile Molly felt ruffled, disarranged, more enticed by the idea of seeing Raoul than she'd have cared to admit to anyone. That being the case, she knew, she'd do well to stay put at home. But there was such a thing as family loyalty. Siobhan had never asked her for help before.

"I feel as if I *should* go," Molly said as the last rosy streaks of color in the sky were swallowed up by encroaching night. "You said it yourself, Aunt Rosie. Siobhan isn't the sort to cry wolf."

Rosie O'Meara's sharp blue eyes glittered as she studied her niece's profile in the dusk. "You must do as you think best," she advised. "I only hope you won't be flattered or cajoled into doing something you'll regret. I can't help feeling Siobhan's up to no good, though I don't have the slightest proof. If you decide to fly to France, why not let Matt go along? He could use a vacation and you'd enjoy each other's company. Since Siobhan's willing to buy you a ticket, I'll be happy to pay for his.''

Ultimately, with a bit of transatlantic coaxing from Siobhan and the nagging of her own conscience that her sister shouldn't be made to suffer for her unfortunate crush, Molly decided to make the trip. To her relief, Matt was able to accompany her. The bishop who was his superior didn't raise any objections. She knew it would be easier to face Raoul and her strong-willed sister with Matt at her side.

Two weeks from the day Siobhan's telegram had arrived, Molly and Matt were airborne over the Atlantic, watching the sun refract in a giant fisherman's net of diamonds from the restless blue-black waters below.

Though she wasn't quite sure why, Molly had neglected to inform Siobhan their brother was making the trip. She had the oddest premonition her older sister wouldn't be pleased to see him. That's ridiculous, she thought. Siobhan and Matt have always been close. But she still couldn't shake the notion.

Somewhere over midocean she asked the stewardess for a blanket and pillow. Most of her fellow passengers seemed to be dozing. Meanwhile Matt was reading his obligatory daily office. She decided she might as well sleep. But it didn't work out that way. The release of a dream state continued to elude her though she deliberately relaxed her body inch by inch. Again and again, her thoughts returned to Siobhan, Raoul and their troubled marriage.

I have a feeling I'm getting in over my head on this mission of mercy, she thought uneasily, shifting position in the roomy, first-class seat. But it was too late to change her mind and cling to the safety of her own life.

They landed at Roissy-Charles de Gaulle at about 4:00 p.m., the equivalent of 10:00 a.m. in Palm Beach. Though Matt had snatched a few hours' sleep, Molly felt as if she had a hangover. She cursed herself for hoping she wouldn't have to face Raoul until she'd had some rest to erase the shadows beneath her eyes.

To her relief, Siobhan was unaccompanied as she waited for them at the gate. Briefly her older sister's face betrayed a lack of recognition. Then she grinned appreciatively at the curvaceous, grown-up figure Molly cut in her blue-violet linen designer suit. "Little sister," she murmured with pleasure, enveloping Molly in her perfumed embrace. "You've grown up and then some!"

"I should hope so. I'm twenty-three."

Siobhan didn't seem to hear her reply. Instead, she was staring at Matt as he emerged from the jetway in his priestly garb. *You didn't tell me he was coming,* her darting green eyes accused.

Seconds later Siobhan's expression of dismay and chagrin might have been a mirage. "Matt!" she exclaimed, hugging him in turn. "What a wonderful surprise! The three of us are going to have such fun together!"

Molly and Matt exchanged a clandestine look. *Fun?* Molly couldn't help asking herself. Is *that* what this is all about? She could see that Matt was similarly mystified. Knowing Siobhan, she didn't expect her older sister would tell them what sort of help she wanted until she was good and ready—not a moment before.

Thanks to eleven years as a Parisienne who moved in the very best circles, Siobhan spoke excellent French. She shepherded them through customs with her usual flair.

"Père Fitzwilliam et Mme Dunlap n'ont rien à déclarer," she announced, introducing herself to the agent as Comtesse Beaulieu de Montfort and pouring on the charm. *"Est-ce que c'est possible d'être vite? Mon mari est très pressé et il nous attend, vous comprenez."*

Smitten, the short, middle-aged man beamed at her. *"Mais il serait mon plaisir, madame,"* he answered, waving them through.

Thanks to her college French, Molly was able to translate. Siobhan had asked the man to be quick because her husband, an important and busy political figure, was waiting for them. She swallowed nervously. The moment they exited the terminal, it seemed, she'd find herself face-to-face with Raoul.

But Siobhan's broodingly handsome husband was nowhere to be seen. Instead, as they stepped out on the sidewalk trailed by a porter with their luggage, a classic Mercedes convertible pulled smoothly to the curb. The car's top was down and its elegant cream-colored fenders appeared freshly waxed. Tanned and handsome with longish sun-streaked hair, the driver looked like a wealthy tennis bum in his early thirties. He gazed uncertainly at Matt, then Siobhan, and got out from behind the wheel.

In the convertible's back seat, another man and a woman were also giving Matt puzzled looks. Clearly they hadn't expected a priest to join their party.

With a sidelong glance at their chauffeur-to-be, Siobhan introduced him as Marc St. Onge, an old family friend. "Marc, this is Molly," she said in her composed way. "And our brother Matt. As you may have guessed, I wasn't expecting him."

"It's a great pleasure to meet you," Marc replied in English, shaking each of their hands in turn. "Siobhan has told me so much about you both."

She introduced Marc's companions as he stowed their luggage in the Mercedes's trunk. Sleek, expensively dressed and obviously indolent, Lili Charpentier and Jean-Paul DeBrosse gave Molly and her brother amused, ironic smiles.

"I'm afraid I arranged with Lili, Marc and Jean-Paul to go to the Deux Magots Café for drinks in honor of Molly's arrival," Siobhan said, addressing Matt as they got into the car. "I hope that won't be too dissolute for your taste."

Despite the fact that he drank socially and often attended parties hosted by his parishioners, Molly could see her brother was ill at ease. But, "Lead on," he quipped with a grin, wedging himself into the back seat with his sister's friends. "If worse comes to worst, I can always turn my collar around."

With Molly sandwiched between him and Siobhan, Marc started the Mercedes's deeply purring engine. Breeze ruffled their hair as they slipped into traffic on the autoroute, heading for the heart of the city.

What's going on? Molly asked herself, glancing at Siobhan and then at Marc as they abandoned the suburbs for the gentler ambiance of uniformly classical buildings in soft gradations of gray, an exaltation of chestnut trees in blossom. Can this whole thing be a matchmaking attempt on Siobhan's part? Is that why she's so upset Matt came along?

A sixth sense told her the reasons for Siobhan's displeasure and Marc's presence at the airport wouldn't turn out to be that neat. There was something between Marc and Siobhan, something the wayward redhead didn't want Matt to know about. The private look they'd exchanged and several small, barely perceptible gestures on her sister's part had testified to that.

With a sinking feeling Molly realized they were probably having an affair. I wonder where Raoul fits into this picture, she thought as they crossed the Seine at the Île de la Cité and turned from the Boul' Mich' onto the Boulevard St. Germain. Does he know what's going on? Or is he so absorbed in his work that he doesn't care?

Perhaps Raoul was involved in an illicit relationship of his own. If so, what was she supposed to do about it?

Marc managed to find a parking space in a narrow, picturesque street near the landmark church of St. Germain-des-Prés. Chattering in their native French, a group of small boys dodged the traffic to play ball while an elderly concierge in a faded black apron swept out the doorway of her pension. Loving couples, no doubt students from the university, strolled along the sidewalks with their arms about each other.

Despite her tension over the prospect of seeing Raoul again and the uncertainty of Siobhan's situation, Molly could feel the city's pervasive air of romance seeping into her blood like a low-grade fever. God help me if we have to stay very long, she thought. There's something about this place that would try a nun's resolve.

Exhausted from lack of sleep and shrinking from the whirlpool of emotional crosscurrents she expected to face, Molly allowed Marc St. Onge to pull out a chair for her at one of the Deux Magots's sidewalk tables. If memory served her right, the café-bar had been one of the favorite hangouts of Parisian artists and literati for decades. Hemingway, Picasso, Sartre and Simone de Beauvoir might previously have occupied her seat.

Nearby, a street musician with a cello was playing for the tips thrown by the patrons of the crowded terrace into his instrument case. Sunlight glinted on his red beard and dappled the pavement.

"It was very thoughtful of you to accompany Siobhan to the airport," she said, smiling up at Marc as guilelessly as she could. "I guess Raoul was too busy at the National Assembly to make the trip."

Before he could answer, Siobhan threw him a warning look. Then, apparently satisfied there hadn't been any hidden barbs in Molly's remark, she gave her auburn tresses a rueful shake.

"Raoul is *always* busy," she complained in a tone that suggested she was being a good sport about it. "He's become a Gallic version of that great American business and political institution, the workaholic. I'm afraid you may not get to see him for several days. He's scheduled to leave this afternoon on a three-day jaunt to the Loire *département* he represents."

Simultaneously relieved and disappointed, Molly allowed Marc to order her an aperitif. Somehow I can't imagine Raoul timing his absence to coincide with the arrival of one of Siobhan's family members, she thought. His manners have always been perfect, and he was such an attentive host when Aunt Rosie and I visited six years ago.

But perhaps Raoul's business trips had become so commonplace that they hardly merited attention these days. Whatever the case, he'd done her a tremendous favor by leaving town. Without his presence to put her on her guard, she'd be able to turn her full attention to her sister's welfare.

* * *

An hour and a half later they were dropping off Lili and Jean-Paul at the former's chic apartment building, and Marc was driving them across the Pont d'Iena to that bastion of the old aristocracy, the sixteenth arrondissement. Set amid the leafy splendor of the Villa Montmorency, the de Montforts' elegant eighteenth-century mansion was situated *entre court et jardin*—between a cobbled courtyard and an emerald expanse of lawn landscaped in the style of Le Notre. Marc St. Onge drove through the open grilled-iron gate with the air of a frequent visitor. As if he'd been anxiously awaiting their arrival, a uniformed manservant appeared to carry in their bags.

"Will you stay for dinner?" Siobhan asked Marc as he opened the car door for them. "As I mentioned, Raoul will be absent. But the rest of the family will be joining us, I suppose."

He laughed as if at a private joke. "Thanks anyway, pet. But I'm not up to coping with your sister-in-law at the moment. Besides, Catherine's expecting me. Have fun at the opera tonight."

Opera? Molly winced. He's got to be kidding. What I need is a good night's sleep! With a frown, she considered the rest of Marc's response. During her visit six years earlier, she hadn't liked Raoul's sister, Marie-Claude, very much either. She'd seemed so bitter and watchful, as if poised to sow the seeds of discord whenever she could.

"Who's Catherine?" she asked, admiring the Louis XV mirrors and inlaid marble tiles of the foyer.

Siobhan smiled with suppressed amusement at the question. "Marc's wife, of course," she answered. "I might add she has a thing for Raoul."

"Did I hear my name mentioned?"

Without their noticing it, the double doors to one of the exquisitely furnished salons that flanked the hall had opened. Handsome as ever in a slubbed gray silk-linen suit and dark blue tie, Raoul was standing there. Molly's heart skipped a beat, then hammered against her ribs. A gasp of astonishment had died in her throat.

"I thought you were going down to Blois," Siobhan posited after a moment.

"I changed my mind."

His mouth curving with ironic humor, he stepped forward to greet them. Not pausing to kiss his wife, he shook Matt's hand and then raised Molly's to his lips.

"Welcome to Paris, Moira Kathleen Dunlap," he murmured, his voice deep and faintly rough, like velvet stroked against the grain. "I shouldn't wonder if you take the city by storm."

Rendered speechless by the compliment and awash in the physical sensations even the slightest contact with him seemed able to call forth, Molly stood transfixed. She felt as if his light-drenched gaze could probe her most carefully guarded secrets.

Chapter Two

To Raoul, Molly's presence was like a fresh breeze in the house. She reminded him of gentleness, modesty and devotion—a whole host of old-fashioned virtues he hadn't thought about for years. This is what I gave up, he thought, when I chased after Siobhan so long ago: the right to pursue happiness with a woman like this.

She was Siobhan's sister and naturally he'd never allow himself to think of her as anything else. Yet in that instant she represented everything he'd missed in his marriage and long since stopped dreaming about.

Standing there so shy and hesitant with her lips softly parted and her big brown eyes luminous in their eloquence, she symbolized everything that, for him, was permanently out of reach. A typical Frenchman, he supposed, would try to inveigle her into an affair. But that wasn't his style. And anyway, one didn't *have* affairs with a woman like Molly. One slipped a wedding ring on her finger and cherished her for the rest of her days.

She was already wearing a ring, the badge of her recent widowhood. Her tragically brief marriage to a American military officer hadn't been a happy one, or so he'd been told. So why did she continue to wear his diamond? Did she cherish his memory that much? Or was it to warn off other men?

All these thoughts and feelings flitted through Raoul's mind in the slight pause that Molly made no move to fill. Barely a trace of them showed in his face. With the polish of long practice he regained his equilibrium. It wouldn't do to have Siobhan laughing at him. Or his sharp-eyed brother-in-law trying to read his mind.

"I insist both of you consider me at your service while you're here," he added, relinquishing Molly's hand. "After your long trip, I'm sure you'll want to go upstairs and change. Dinner will be served in three-quarters of an hour."

Glancing at her sister, Molly saw that her poise, too, had faltered. "I didn't know you'd be home and I was planning to take them to *La Bohème* tonight," Siobhan said, addressing Raoul. "Luciano Pavarotti is singing the lead."

"Take *them*? Then you knew Matt was coming."

"Actually, no..."

He gave her a sardonic smile. "Not to worry. I'll simply phone ahead for extra tickets."

"Then...you're coming with us?"

"But of course, my love. It's been much too long since Molly and Matt have paid us a visit...not to mention the last time you and I went out together."

* * *

Molly let herself shake a little when she gained the privacy of her room. Seeing Raoul had proved even more difficult than she'd expected. The latent power of him, so strong, had surrounded her like a force field. With his dark good looks, faultless manners and propensity for saying and doing the unexpected, he was the most fascinating man she had ever met.

I can't let him get to me like that again, she vowed. When he kissed my hand, I acted like a thunderstruck child. She only prayed Matt and Siobhan hadn't noticed. She wasn't sure how to prevent the same thing from happening again, short of avoiding her sister's extraordinary husband altogether.

Kicking off her shoes and removing her outer clothing, Molly stretched out in her lace-trimmed slip on the silk-satin coverlet of her bed. She was as upset by the obvious tension between Raoul and Siobhan as she was over her own unseemly behavior. Apparently their marriage was in even worse shape than she'd guessed. Overwhelmed as she'd been by Raoul's physical and emotional presence, she hadn't missed Siobhan's discomfort or the sarcastic way he'd spoken to her. She'd felt a distinct twinge of embarrassment at his pointed reference to the fact that they spent very little time together.

Yet she was too wise to her sister's ways to consider Raoul the only culprit. Seeing Siobhan with Marc that afternoon had been enough to make Molly brand her as co-conspirator in their marital troubles. When Matt had turned up at the airport, Siobhan had moved a bit too quickly to put an innocent face on things. She'd be on her best behavior now, Molly guessed. Yet the connection was there, without a doubt. Unless she was very much mistaken, her sister and Marc St. Onge were lovers. She didn't understand how Siobhan could carry on that way if she wanted her marriage to last.

I wonder what Matt thinks of all this, Molly asked herself wearily, allowing her eyes to close for a moment. I hope I have a chance to talk to him before we go downstairs.

But there wasn't any rush. She had a few minutes to rest, at least twenty-four hours to assess the situation and almost two weeks to do whatever was expected of her. Meanwhile the big, canopied bed felt so soft, so comfortable. And she was so tired. Every muscle in her body ached.

Gradually her mind drifted back to a time when they'd all lived together in the big house on London Road in Duluth. Matt and Siobhan had been college undergraduates then, Molly a third-grader. Yet as memory merged with the images of sleep, she saw them all as adults, including herself. In her dream, when she emerged from the sunlit depths of her parents' swimming pool to shake gleaming droplets of water from her sleek, dark hair, it seemed the most natural thing in all the world that Raoul should be waiting by the pool apron, waiting to kiss her hand.

Seated in front of a Moorish bust and a seventeenth-century Italian tapestry at the head of the de Montforts' sumptuously set dinner table, Raoul let his glance stray to Molly's empty place. The maid had informed them Mme Dunlap was fast asleep. He'd agreed with his mother that it was best not to disturb her. But he missed her presence, more than he'd expected to.

I wonder what she'll make of us, he thought, his eyes roving over the priceless settings of Meissen porcelain and Baccarat crystal that had been in his family for generations before coming to rest on Siobhan's lovely face. Molly was so young the last time she visited here. Yet even then she must have seen beneath the surface of our relationship and guessed that something wasn't right.

Would she be able to read Siobhan at that moment?

He wanted to raise his glass in tribute to the imitation Siobhan was giving of a caring, affectionate wife. You should have been an actress, *chèrie,* he told her silently. You have the talent for it. Tonight you deserve an American Academy Award.

Since coming to France eleven years ago, Siobhan had known which side her bread was buttered on. Sensing the power and implacability of Gabrielle de Montfort, she'd behaved toward his mother with unfailing courtesy and respect.

He hadn't blamed Siobhan for assessing Marie-Claude as a mean-spirited sneak and treating her accordingly. Though he was more polite to his sister than Siobhan was, he felt that way about Marie-Claude, too.

What had caught him by surprise soon after their marriage was the evolution of Siobhan's attitude toward himself. During their courtship, she'd been admiring and oh, so sweet though she'd refused to let him make love to her. Like a fool, he'd imagined she was a virgin. It hadn't upset him that much when he found out otherwise. He'd guessed that she withheld her favors to lure him into marriage but he hadn't minded that, either. Believing himself in love, he'd been all too willing to satisfy her every craving and make the most of her experience in bed.

Yet even in their first days as a married couple he'd begun to feel her slipping away. In a burst of temper she'd described their vows as a kind of prison. Flirting outrageously with other men, she'd accused him alternately of not caring whether she cheated on him and of taking a lover himself. It hadn't been long before he'd had proof positive she was having affairs.

Yet she'd continued to want him, particularly when she'd suspected there was somebody else even though that had never been the case. At first it had been difficult for him to refuse. But with time it had become easier. The kind of arrangement she seemed to want might be commonplace and even fashionable in their social circles, but it wasn't his style. The older he got, the more he wanted something solid and lasting in his life. Eventually he'd become inured, both to Siobhan's charms and her transgressions, and buried himself in his work.

She'd never leave him, of course—probably fight him like the very devil if he ever threatened to leave her. Divorce was out of the question, insofar as both their families were concerned. He knew Siobhan had derived a tremendous kick from being a *comtesse* since his father died. She liked spending the de Montfort money, too, while tenaciously hanging on to her own inheritance.

Tonight she was gazing at him with stars in her eyes. He didn't doubt they were strictly for Matt's benefit. But he had to admit that, in the soft light from the room's heirloom candelabra and crystal chandelier, her performance was very convincing. He wondered if his brother-in-law had been taken in.

Marie-Claude certainly wasn't, he realized. Sipping morosely at her wine, Raoul's older, unmarried sister watched Siobhan as though waiting to pounce. Though their mother's features were arranged in their usual attitude of aristocratic negligence, he guessed she too was curious about what was afoot. Meanwhile the conversation about his work in the National Assembly and the problems France was experiencing just then with international terrorism flowed without interruption around the table.

It was dark outside when Molly awoke to Siobhan's light touch on her shoulder. "You must have been awfully tired, kitten," her sister said.

Molly blinked. "Oh my gosh! Dinner!"

"We went ahead without you. Maman decreed that you needed your rest."

'Maman' was Raoul's mother, the widowed Comtesse Gabrielle. If Molly remembered correctly, her word was unwritten law in the household.

"Thank heaven for that," she whispered. "I'm so embarrassed I fell asleep. What about the opera? I hope you haven't canceled your plans on my behalf."

Siobhan smiled, her green eyes lazy. "The plans were for you," she said. "There's still time to go if you're feeling up to it. Why not get up and splash a little cool water on your face? I'll have Martine bring you some tea and toast."

For the first time, Molly became aware of her sister's gown. A frivolous confection of beads and silk fringe that ended at midthigh, it had haute couture written all over it. Yet it was undeniably sexy and frivolous. The color matched her eyes and contrasted sharply with her tumble of auburn curls.

"I gather this is a dress-up occasion," Molly said dryly, getting to her feet. "Give me a couple of minutes and I'll attempt to do you proud."

She came downstairs in a modestly cut, unadorned column of a dress in silk-blend silver lamé she'd chosen from the shop. She wore matching pumps. A simple diamond barrette held her smooth, dark hair in place. Siobhan's baby sister has definitely become a woman,

Raoul noted as he held her wrap and then met her tremulous gaze. Supposedly her pilot husband had cheated on her. Even in such a wicked world, he didn't understand how that could be the case.

The Paris Opera, with its rococo chandeliers and sweeping grand staircase crowned by caryatids, was every bit as impressive as Molly remembered. Now that she was rested and fully awake, she found herself rising to the occasion. Inside she might be trembling at Raoul's touch but she'd never let him know it. Out of loyalty to Siobhan and her own strict moral code, she'd use every contact with him as another occasion to harden her heart.

To her surprise, Raoul led them to a private box. So that business about phoning for tickets was just his little joke, Molly realized. He was mocking Siobhan, knowing we'd find out the truth sooner or later. But though she didn't like the mordant streak she detected in him, she couldn't fault him for it if he knew his wife and Marc St. Onge were involved.

Molly managed to put the de Montforts and their tangled personal relationships on hold at least temporarily when the curtain rose. An opera buff and an ardent Pavarotti fan, she loved *La Bohème*'s poignance and grandeur. In her opinion, both libretto and score contained just enough frivolity and humor to make the final scene infinitely more tragic.

She was carried out of herself when Pavarotti's voice soared in the first act's proud, tender aria, *"Che gelida manina."* His magnificent tenor completely filled the great opera house's baroque, grandiloquent space. Yet her pleasure was tinged with sadness, because she knew what was going to happen to Mimì, the female character he was singing to. Overcome with emotion, Molly clasped her brother's hand, tears glinting against her lashes.

Equally moved, Matt gave her a gentle pat.

A moment later, her gaze clashed with Raoul's. *I know what you're feeling,* his beautiful eyes seemed to whisper. *Love doesn't always turn out as we want it to.* She had the sudden conviction he wished things didn't have to be like that.

Stop, she ordered herself, forcing her attention back to the stage. You're not a mind reader. It's the height of insanity, ascribing emotions to Raoul that he doesn't feel.

During the intermission she was all but silent, despite the fact that Matt had disappeared to the restroom and Siobhan left them for several minutes to speak to friends. Fetching her a Perrier as if he guessed she wouldn't want alcohol with so little food in her stomach, Raoul did his best to keep up a semblance of conversation. His smile pleasant and his eyes once more unreadable, he spoke knowledgeably about Puccini's work, Pavarotti's performance and the history of the Paris Opera itself.

It was quite late when they returned to the de Montfort residence. Thanking Siobhan and Raoul for a marvelous time, Molly excused herself almost immediately and went up to her room. She was already wearing her white lace nightgown and brushing her hair at a small, elegantly appointed dressing table when Siobhan knocked and entered. Sprawling with apparent ease in a nearby chair, Molly's sister was still wearing her spiky sandals and beaded dress.

As she turned to speak with her, Molly thought she detected a whiff of brandy on Siobhan's breath. But if her sister had been drinking, it hadn't relaxed her. Siobhan seemed edgy, even tense. Maybe she's finally going to divulge her reasons for dragging me halfway around the world, Molly thought. I can't wait.

"Tonight was wonderful," she said, giving Siobhan a moment to arrange her thoughts. "I've never heard Pavarotti sing before, except on television and compact disc, of course. We're fairly civilized in Palm Beach, but nothing can top Paris for sheer cultural wealth."

"I'm glad you enjoyed it, baby sis."

Pensively Siobhan examined her manicure, causing the huge diamond Raoul had given her to sparkle in the soft light from several rose-shaded lamps. Watching her, Molly held her silver-backed hairbrush in abeyance.

"I realize you haven't been here long," Siobhan went on finally. "But I'm wondering what you think of our situation."

"You mean . . . yours and Raoul's?"

"That's the one I'm referring to."

It was a ticklish question, to say the least. Molly couldn't think of a diplomatic answer. "If I had to guess, I'd say things aren't going very well," she admitted.

"You'd be right."

For several seconds, silence reigned in the room. Molly waited, a painful sensation gripping her chest.

"I've found out I can't have children," Siobhan revealed in a rush, her hands twisting suddenly in her lap. "Raoul . . . or perhaps I should say his mother . . . wants an heir . . . for the title, you know, to keep her late husband's nephew from inheriting. She's even threatened she'll push him to seek an annulment unless something can be done. In case you haven't noticed, Raoul's only interested in his work. It's Gabrielle who rules this household. I'm terrified he'll go along with what she wants, dump me for some nubile young thing who can give him the son he wants."

"Oh, Sib! In this day and age . . . you can't mean it!" Her hairbrush falling to the floor, Molly flung her arms around her sister's neck. How could she have been so mistaken about the essential goodness of her sister's husband?

"Promise me you won't tell Matt or Aunt Rosie," Siobhan begged in a muffled voice. "I don't want them to know what the situation is just yet."

"Of course I won't if you don't want me to. But you know they love you. Maybe there's something they could do to help." Her heart aching, Molly held her sister close.

"You're the only one who can help me, Molly."

For some reason, Siobhan's words had a chilling effect. "I don't see how," Molly protested worriedly, drawing back to search her sister's face. "I can talk to Raoul, of course. But there's no guarantee he'll listen...."

"I don't want you to *talk* to him, kitten. I want you to have his baby."

The shock waves of Siobhan's incredible pronouncement reverberated like thunder in the quiet room. Molly gaped at her sister as if she were some stranger who had just proposed a suicide pact. The idea Siobhan had voiced was so utterly outrageous, so unthinkable, Molly wondered if she'd lost her mind.

"You . . . you can't mean . . ." she choked out.

"Ah, but I do," Siobhan answered calmly. "It's the only thing that will save my marriage."

"Then it will simply have to fail!" Jumping to her feet, Molly snatched up her matching robe. In a whirl of silk and lace, she started for the door.

As quickly Siobhan caught her by the arm. "Where are you going?" she demanded. "You promised . . ."

"Not to tell anybody?" Tears of anguish filled Molly's eyes. "I didn't guarantee to keep silent about anything like this!"

"So you're going to run and tell Matt, just like you did when you were a child!" Siobhan's voice was harshly critical and she softened it with obvious effort. "Don't be a silly goose," she added more gently. "Sit down and hear me out. I'm not suggesting you have sex with Raoul."

Molly stared. "What, then?"

"I want you to get pregnant by him. But not in the usual way. Surely you've heard of artificial insemination."

"Well, of course I have." Still poised for flight, Molly hesitated. "But it's crazy even to think . . ."

"Please . . . sit down," Siobhan urged, relaxing her hold on Molly's arm. "You've come all the way to Paris because, in theory at least, you were willing to help me out of a tight spot. Let me tell you what I have in mind."

Feeling like a sacrificial lamb about to be led to the slaughter, Molly sank down on the stool before her dressing table. Siobhan can't make you do anything you don't want to do, she reminded herself with a shudder. You might as well find out just how crazy she is.

Siobhan took a deep breath as if she felt the first and most strenuous objections provoked by her radical request had been successfully laid to rest. She took Molly's hands in hers, apparently sensing a need to maintain physical contact.

"I want you to be a surrogate mother for us, Molly," she explained, her green eyes delving deep into Molly's brown ones for some glimmer of sympathy and rapport. "Any child of yours and Raoul's would have the same basic genetic makeup as one he and I would have conceived together. You would carry the baby for nine months but we would be its legal parents. It would be a gift of love to us. The breach in our marriage would be healed."

Molly was totally flabbergasted by the concept. "You mean...have a baby and just give it up like that?" she whispered. "I couldn't...not even for you!"

Undeterred by Molly's distress, Siobhan forged ahead. With her usual devastating accuracy, she probed for a tender spot. "You'd be the child's aunt," she reasoned. "Plus it would give you a chance to experience motherhood...something you'll never do otherwise if you mean what you say about not getting married again."

I'm only twenty-three, Molly thought. In a lifetime of surprises and reverses, I could change my mind. Or decide to adopt as a single parent. But she had to admit the idea of growing a baby beneath her heart appealed to her deepest womanly instincts.

Growing *Raoul's* baby beneath her heart. Involuntarily her hand went to her stomach. "No!" she exclaimed, panic-stricken at the unwanted thrill of vulnerability that brought a flush to her cheeks. "I couldn't. The Church doesn't approve of surrogate motherhood and I don't, either. Look at all the trouble it's caused in other cases."

Perhaps realizing she wasn't on solid ground, Siobhan didn't exactly argue. "I can see your point," she admitted. "And it's a valid one. But this would be different. You wouldn't be *paid* to have the baby. It would be a totally selfless act. Please, Molly... I know your first instinct is to refuse. And maybe your second one, too. But promise me you'll give it some thought."

Regarding her sister in consternation, Molly didn't know what to say. I could consider a request like this until doomsday, she told herself, and my answer would be the same. "Does Raoul know you planned to propose something like this?" she asked suddenly.

The question appeared to throw Siobhan off balance for a moment. "I didn't want to broach the subject with him until after I'd talked to you," she admitted.

I'm not surprised to hear it, Molly countered silently. She didn't reply.

Always attentive to the subtle nuances involved in any negotiation, Siobhan chose that moment to say goodnight. "We'll talk more about this tomorrow if you're willing," she said, planting a tentative kiss on Molly's forehead. "After crossing six time zones, you must be dying for some sleep."

Molly grimaced at her belated solicitude. "Too bad you didn't think of that before dropping your bombshell at bedtime," she countered.

"Sorry." Siobhan had the grace to look abashed. "You're right, of course. It's just that the chance to recapture what Raoul and I once had means so much to me. I couldn't wait."

Molly closed her eyes briefly after Siobhan had left the room. She had a buzzing feeling in her ears and a headache had begun to throb at her temples. She felt sick, literally hollow inside at having been forced to face such an outrageous imposition.

My God, she thought, if I'd had the slightest notion what was on Siobhan's mind, I'd never have left Florida. Since she'd come to Paris, however, she had to find some way to refuse her sister without causing a serious, perhaps permanent, family rift.

Yet though granting Siobhan's plea was totally out of the question, Molly couldn't bring herself to be angry— even if that might have given her some additional energy to deal with the situation. Whether or not it was all an act, her sister had sounded genuinely desperate. She'd seemed convinced her marriage would fail if Molly didn't cooperate.

For the first time Molly wondered if Siobhan was pretending to have an affair with Marc in the hope of making Raoul jealous and winning back his affection. She supposed it was a possibility. Instinct argued otherwise. Siobhan's discomfort at Matt's searching gaze had been all too real.

After giving it some thought, Molly decided she was under no obligation to keep the subject of their conversation from her brother. Divide and conquer—that's probably how Sib plans to push this through, she thought. Well, it's not going to work. Aunt Rosie asked Matt to come along in case things turned out to be more than I could handle and that's just what has happened.

But it was too late at that hour to seek Matt's advice. By now, she guessed, her brother would be fast asleep, regrouping in order to say Mass the following morning as arranged at the de Montforts' parish church.

Realizing she'd have to rise early to catch him before he left the house, Molly knew she'd better get to sleep herself. Yet how was she supposed to manage that, with so many disturbing thoughts racing through her head?

She set her travel alarm for 5:30 a.m. and placed it on her night table. Then, halving one of the little blue tablets her doctor had given her at the time of Kirk's death, she downed one portion with some water. Something—perhaps a premonition of trouble—had made her toss the sleeping pills in her cosmetic bag. Slipping between the sheets of her canopied bed, she tried to think of everything that needed doing at the shop in lieu of dwelling on Siobhan's problems as she waited for sleep to come.

* * *

Dressed in a softly gathered peach-colored silk linen skirt, matching cotton sweater and flats, and wearing a printed silk kerchief tied beneath her chin, Molly looked like a schoolgirl as she fell into step with Matt the following morning. "We have a problem," she said as they strode down the quiet residential street toward the church's gray stone edifice.

His black cassock fluttered in the breeze as he turned to give her a searching look. "What is it?" he asked.

"Siobhan has found out she can't have children. She wants me to be a surrogate mother for her and Raoul. She claims that, if I refuse, their marriage will be over."

Matt let out a most unpriestly oath. "God forgive me," he muttered as if to wipe his slate clean, "but I couldn't help it. That's the craziest, most obscenely self-ish thing she's ever tried to pull. Of course you said *no*."

"I explained something like that would go against my deepest convictions. She . . . didn't want me to tell you about it."

"She wouldn't, of course."

Plainly relieved by Molly's answer, Matt resumed his pace. Surely he hadn't believed Molly was so in awe of Siobhan she'd actually consider such a scheme?

A moment later they reached the church's front steps. Matt paused before going off to the sacristy to don his vestments. "You were right to share this with me," he said, squeezing Molly's hand. "I'll offer this Mass for a reconciliation between Siobhan and Raoul. But it's up to them to bring it about, not you. Try to remember that."

Back at the de Montfort household, Siobhan had risen early, too. Though she usually skipped the day's first meal in favor of lying abed until around 11:00 a.m., she joined her surprised mother-in-law in the mansion's breakfast room at a quarter to eight.

"You're looking energetic this morning," Gabrielle de Montfort remarked, giving her a speculative look.

"I wanted to talk to you," Siobhan said forthrightly in her flawless French, "without Raoul or Marie-Claude present."

"Very well." The senior *comtesse* calmly buttered a croissant.

"It's about the fact that I can't seem to conceive," Siobhan added, gaining the older woman's full attention at once. "And, if I may put it bluntly, your threat that you'll urge Raoul to seek an annulment. I asked my sister to come here to Paris in the hope she'd agree to act as a surrogate mother for us. I know the Church frowns on any such arrangement, just as it frowns on divorce. But a child Molly would bear to Raoul would have essentially the same genetic makeup as a child of ours...certainly on its father's side. If it turned out to be a boy, there wouldn't be any further difficulty about the inheritance."

Maintaining her reputation for unflappability, Siobhan's mother-in-law didn't speak for a moment. Then, "What does Molly say to all this?" she asked.

"So far she's refused me. I haven't told Raoul. First I wanted to ask for your support."

Outside the door to the breakfast room, unseen by either Siobhan or Gabrielle, Marie-Claude was listening. Her pasty face took on an expression of malicious pleasure. Without waiting to hear any more and risk revealing herself, she hurried back up the stairs.

Several minutes later, Raoul came storming down in her stead. His appearance brought the conversation in the breakfast room to an abrupt halt. "Marie-Claude just came to me with the most extraordinary tale," he ground out, glancing angrily from his wife to his mother and back again. "I trust you'll be able to set things straight!"

Raoul was roaring out the front gate of the de Montfort property in his Citroën when Matt and Molly returned from church. Catching sight of them, he braked to a stop. "Get in," he ordered Molly, his face contorted with fury. "I must talk with you."

"Not so fast." Protectively Matt put one arm about Molly's shoulders. "You haven't any right..."

"I'll be okay." With her soft heart, Molly had sensed the pain beneath Raoul's rage. Instinctively she wanted to ease it. Though the thought had terrified her before, she wasn't afraid to be alone with him now—or talk with him about his and Siobhan's situation.

"If you're sure..." Matt said doubtfully.

Molly nodded. "We'll be back in a little while."

She got into the car. Shoving it into gear, Raoul took off like a shot. She'd always guessed a passionate nature lay beneath his carefully controlled facade but she'd never seen it displayed before. She felt attracted by it and at the same time repelled. Clearly he'd learned of Siobhan's request and felt in some way humiliated by it. But if he'd really go along with Gabrielle's insistence that he dump her sister unless she could manage to bear him a child, he'd forfeited her sympathy and respect.

Determined to find out the truth, Molly folded her hands, resisting the urge to clutch at the armrest as they rounded a corner from the Avenue Mozart onto the busy Rue du Ranelagh. She knew better than to press Raoul at the moment. If she waited, perhaps his temper would subside and she might learn something. In the meantime, he apparently needed to disobey the Paris traffic laws to the utmost in order to get the monkey that was tormenting him off his back.

Crossing the Seine, they sped up the Quai Branly past the Tour Eiffel and the Pont de l'Alma. Gradually the volume of traffic forced them to slow their pace. Raoul glanced at her, his tawny eyes unreadable. "I know a quiet place in this hive of a city," he said. "Would you be willing to walk with me there?"

"I suppose so," Molly said.

Raoul's sanctuary turned out to be the courtyard of the Musée de Cluny in one of the oldest parts of Paris. He didn't suggest they go inside to see the fifteenth-century tapestries or the museum's superb collection of Limoges enamels. Instead their destination turned out to be the mossy brick-and-stone ruin of a second-century Roman bath.

"I don't think I've ever touched anything so ancient," Molly whispered, resting her hand on a wall that felt cool despite the patch of blue sky overhead and the warmth of the morning sunlight.

"Paris is more than two thousand years old," Raoul replied. "I come here sometimes when I need to gain that perspective."

Not answering him, Molly dusted off the top of a low stone ledge and took a seat.

"You must be full of questions, yet you don't ask them," Raoul noted.

"I want to see what you'll tell me of your own accord."

He shook his head. "You're an unusual woman, do you know that? But then I suspected you would be, long ago."

It was the first time they'd been alone together. The compliment pierced her heart with a bittersweet stab of longing. What if she'd been old enough for him when he was twenty-seven and a bachelor? What if she'd met him first?

He'd been so much in love with Siobhan on their wedding day. Resolutely Molly pushed away the might-have-beens. Maybe that love could be resurrected. She could only hope.

As she watched, a stubbornness she hadn't seen before appeared in Raoul's face. "Thanks to Marie-Claude, I've learned of the sacrifice my wife is proposing you make for us," he said in a voice that was suddenly all business. "I consider Siobhan's selfishness in asking such a thing to be a disgrace and I apologize on her behalf. Unfortunately, she has already broached the topic to my mother, a strong-willed woman who is deeply concerned that I should get an heir. Maman is disposed to look on the idea with favor. She has a way of getting what she wants."

There was a pause in which Molly began to realize the full extent of the mess Siobhan had plunged them into.

"The best thing you could do for all concerned," Raoul added, his beautiful eyes going hard as topaz, "would be to leave Paris immediately and not return."

Chapter Three

Though Molly knew he was right, Raoul's words left a bitter taste. She felt repudiated, summarily banished from his presence. Henceforth, it seemed, she'd no longer be welcome in the de Montfort household. Already struggling with the guilt she felt for getting mixed up in his and Siobhan's private affairs, she began to wonder if Raoul blamed her for helping hatch her sister's ill-advised scheme.

As they got back into the Citroën she reminded herself he hadn't accused her of anything. On the contrary, he'd apologized for his wife's behavior. He appeared to be furious with Siobhan for embarrassing her, not to mention placing her at the center of a family controversy.

Far from ostracizing me, Raoul's giving me the best possible advice, she thought more calmly as they recrossed the Seine into the aristocratic arrondissement where he lived. It was a mistake for me to come to Paris—

and it would be an even greater one to stay. She vowed she'd return to Florida on the next available flight.

Her lashes partly lowered, Molly cast a surreptitious glance at Raoul's firmly hewn profile. Seething with anger and sunk in the torment of his unhappy marriage, he'd never guess the haunting might-have-beens that would follow her back to the States. She hadn't given him any reason to suspect the regret that might overcome her at the thought she could have had his baby.

The urge to carry Raoul's child, which had sprung full-blown from the deepest part of herself the moment Siobhan had put forth her outrageous proposal, was an alluring but dangerous weed. It had to be pulled up by the roots and cast into the fire. Never mind that its eradication would leave a desert in its place.

Well, what did you expect? Molly asked herself angrily. Nothing's changed. You're still a twenty-three-year-old widow who in all likelihood will never remarry. You've simply had one more reminder that the man you want is permanently out of reach.

Her salvation would continue to be her work. Still, seated in such close proximity to Raoul that she could feel the magnetic pull of him and catch an occasional whiff of his tangy, masculine scent, she knew things were different. The childish infatuation she'd contracted like a virus when she was twelve had ripened into something much more profound. She loved Raoul now as a woman loved a man though she'd never admit it to anyone and fight it with all her strength.

She remembered suddenly she hadn't asked Raoul what she considered her most pressing question. "Is it true you might press Siobhan for an annulment because of her inability to have children?" she said, shattering the silence between them.

Raoul set his jaw. "Nothing like that has ever been mentioned," he replied stiffly, not really answering her at all.

Brakes squealing, they drew up at the de Montfort *porte-cochère*. Before Molly could get out of the car, Raoul had come around to open the door for her. His dark brows knit together in a frown, he extended his hand.

Accepting it a trifle hesitantly, she emerged. To touch him was agony. And pure heaven. Putting an ocean between them wouldn't be enough.

Molly had no way of knowing how appealing and vulnerable she looked. Upset as he was himself, Raoul longed to wrap his arms around her and ease the hurt she so plainly felt.

"I'm very sorry any of this had to happen," he said.

Her voice was barely audible. "It wasn't your fault."

Seconds passed as they stood there in the cobbled, formally landscaped courtyard, brown eyes drowning in hazel ones, scarcely a breath apart. Unformed thoughts, parent to words that could never be spoken, brushed the air like angels' wings.

Then Raoul was muttering something about National Assembly business and getting back behind the wheel. Staring after him as he clashed the Citroën's gears and roared out the open gate, Molly felt all but abandoned. Far from giving up, she knew, Siobhan would use every weapon at her command to get her way. If it weren't for Matt, she thought, I'd be facing a hornets' nest alone.

Aristide, the de Montforts' butler, opened the door silently at her approach. To her distress, angry voices reached her ears as she entered the foyer. At the click of her heels on the black-and-gold marble tiles, a door opened. Siobhan rushed out to greet her with Matt in hot pursuit.

Unwilling to submit to another painful round of discussion, Molly averted her face.

"Molly, please!" Siobhan cried, clutching at her hand as she tried to brush past. "We have to talk!"

"I *told* you," Matt interrupted, "her answer is no! Let that be an end to it!"

Never had Molly heard so much anger in her brother's voice. Or seen such fierce determination glittering in Siobhan's eyes. "Matt's right," she whispered, blanching at being the focus of their conflict. "You can ask me until doomsday, Sib. My answer will be the same."

With that, she started up the stairs. Shrugging off Matt's restraining hand, Siobhan moved to follow. "If her mind's made up, there can't be any harm in postmortems," she tossed over her shoulder.

Staring after them in obvious frustration, Matt looked as if he wanted to explode.

Molly dug out her plane ticket as soon as she walked into her room. She was already dialing Air France in the hope of changing her reservation when Siobhan flung herself down on the bed. I'll go ahead with the buying trip as originally planned, Molly told herself, refusing to look at her sister. Keep busy until I can put this whole dreadful mess out of my head.

"I'd like to return to the States tonight, if possible," she explained to the ticket agent who took her call. "Would it be too much trouble to arrange a stopover in New York?"

Fortunately Siobhan chose to remain silent as the agent checked availability on her computer. But the news wasn't good. It looked as if Molly might have some difficulty leaving before her scheduled departure date.

"I'm sorry but the tourist season has already begun, Mme. Dunlap," the ticket agent apologized in her excellent English. "We may not be able to get you a seat right away. If you like, I'll check further and call you back."

Appalled at the thought of having to listen to Siobhan's nagging for another day, Molly gave the agent her number. She hardened her heart as she put down the phone. I'm getting out of here if I have to switch airlines and buy a whole new ticket to do it, she promised herself. Nobody and nothing is going to change my mind.

"You might at least *listen* to me," Siobhan said.

With an exasperated sigh, Molly met her sister's gaze. "What choice do I have?" she countered. "This is your house."

For her to speak to Siobhan that way was completely without precedent. Clearly stunned, her sister made no move to interfere when Molly began removing her belongings from the imposing Louis XV armoire where they'd been placed just the day before and transferring them to her traveling cases.

Yet, true to form, the volatile redhead didn't remain speechless for long. Hugging her slender arms as she sat cross-legged on Molly's bed, Siobhan began softly but urgently to argue her case. Though she didn't phrase it in so many words, she made it plain she believed that, without Molly's cooperation, her marriage to Raoul was doomed.

Finally, Molly'd had enough.

"Let me ask you a question," she interrupted, resting her hands on her hips as she faced her silver-tongued sister. "I warn you it's not a pretty one."

Siobhan's confidence didn't appear to falter. "Go ahead...ask," she said.

"I can't believe you care so much about your marriage that you'll beg me to make an enormous sacrifice to save it, yet continue to carry on an affair with Marc St. Onge behind your husband's back. That *is* what's been happening, isn't it?"

Briefly Siobhan's eyes mirrored the trapped, panic-stricken expression they'd held when Molly had caught her in Dan Rainey's arms the night before her wedding. "Yes," she admitted hoarsely, for once appearing utterly defenseless.

Then she rose to the occasion with something of her usual flair. "It's true," she added. "I turned to Marc when Raoul wouldn't have anything more to do with me. I'm only human, after all. I need warmth and affection. Besides, Raoul's had his flings, too... plenty of them. He's not the saint you might suppose!"

Wincing inwardly, Molly didn't let the distaste she felt show in her face. If Siobhan was speaking the truth, she didn't want to hear it. "I don't have any preconceived notions about your husband," she answered. "I don't know him well enough for that."

Briefly Siobhan was silent as she considered Molly's curt reply. "I know I've behaved badly," she admitted at last. "That, no matter what Raoul has done, the current state of affairs between us is partly my fault. But I promise you, Molly... if you'll do this for me, I'll break it off with Marc. Never have another affair as long as I live. I love Raoul. I don't want to lose him!"

What makes you think you'd be doing *me* a favor by promising to be faithful to your husband? Molly was tempted to ask. That's something you should do in any event. But the guilt of her own unwanted thoughts wouldn't let her put those feelings into words. Meanwhile the idea that Siobhan might mend her ways if she became a mother had created a tiny chink of vulnerability in Molly's armor. I've got to remember what Matt said, she thought. Saving Sib's marriage isn't my responsibility.

"I'm sorry," she answered a bit more gently, returning to her task. "I don't know whether surrogate motherhood is moral or even practical but I do know it's not right for me. I have no intention of bargaining with you over your marriage vows. You and Raoul will have to resolve this problem by yourselves."

Seemingly about to argue the point, Siobhan appeared to think better of it. A moment later, she got up and left the room. But though Molly breathed a sigh of relief, she seriously doubted her sister had given up. She wasn't too surprised when the maid, Martine, knocked at her door and murmured in a deferential voice that the senior Mme la Comtesse would like to see her in the morning room.

Good manners made it a command performance.

"Please tell her I'll be there in a moment," Molly answered, recalling Raoul's remark in the Musée de Cluny courtyard. In his considerable experience, he'd said, "Maman" had a way of getting what she wanted. She wondered if she should ask Matt to accompany her.

It wasn't too difficult to guess what Aunt Rosie would advise. Matt was there to back her up and she'd be wise to take advantage of it. Yet something, a deep-rooted sense of pride, perhaps, whispered that Gabrielle wouldn't respect her if she appeared to need a champion. She decided to go it alone.

Until that afternoon, she and Raoul's rail-thin, supremely elegant mother hadn't exchanged more than a dozen words. To the elder *comtesse*, she suspected, she'd simply been Siobhan's younger sister, an unknown quantity of very little interest. Now all that had changed. As she entered the Frenchwoman's green-and-gilt parlor with its brocade *fauteuils* and priceless Impressionist paintings, she was uncomfortably aware of Gabrielle's calculating gaze.

Seated beside the unlit hearth in a simple black designer dress, Raoul's mother looked utterly self-possessed. Like his, her eyes were a light hazel rimmed with gold but there the similarity ended. Beneath her lashes, all trace of emotion lay shuttered, hidden. The vulnerable, feeling woman within was completely out of reach.

She was, in a word, intimidating. But Molly had conviction on her side. Both Matt and Raoul agreed with her refusal. Determined to appear nonchalant, she waited for the older woman to speak.

"Please...make yourself comfortable, my dear," Gabrielle murmured, motioning her to a chair.

Though doubtless Siobhan had asked her to intercede, the senior *comtesse* had wisely sent her daughter-in-law from the room. Siobhan's volatile style was not her own. Taking a seat as bidden, Molly folded her hands in her lap.

Gabrielle regarded her quizzically for a moment. Then she appeared to come to a decision. "I understand from Siobhan that she's asked you to be a surrogate mother for her and Raoul," she said, going straight to the business at hand. "And that you've refused her, citing as one of your reasons the strong opposition of Holy Mother Church."

Somewhat taken aback by her direct approach, Molly met the older woman's gaze without faltering. "That's true," she said.

"May I say that I see your point?" Gabrielle paused as if allowing her quiet reasonableness the chance to sink in for a moment. "As you know," she went on, "we're all devout Catholics here...well versed in the Church's position."

"Then you can have no quarrel with my reply."

The older woman's graceful, blue-veined hands lay relaxed and motionless on the arms of her chair. If there was a spark of temper in her eyes, Molly didn't catch it.

"For the most part I don't," the *comtesse* agreed. "I believe as you do that hiring out one's womb for pay is morally wrong and demeaning for everyone concerned. But I don't see how that criticism can be leveled at a deed done out of love and loyalty in the bosom of one's own family."

Molly wanted to shake her head in frustration. She might have known Gabrielle would chose to draw the line between love and money as the quickest way of reaching her. It wasn't any secret that Molly worshiped her older siblings, particularly since her parents had died. But did loving someone mean you had to be ready to do anything for them—even if it went against your principles and threatened to cause you a great deal of anguish?

"Am I to understand you don't see anything wrong with what Siobhan's proposing?" she asked.

Gabrielle shrugged, a dismissive gesture that subtly downplayed any sacrifice that might be required on Molly's part. "One can never be completely sure how things will turn out when one is operating in a new theater of human experience," she conceded. "No doubt I'm being selfish. But I'm inclined to think first and foremost of what a child would mean to Raoul. The birth of a son would set his mind at rest about perpetuation of the de Montfort line. As you may know, our family name stretches back more than five centuries."

So do Fitzwilliam, Dunlap and any other you'd care to name, Molly thought. Ultimately we all have the same ancestors. "Siobhan has mentioned it to me a time or two," she said.

The *comtesse* nodded. "Of course I can see there might be some drawbacks for you...."

Let's be honest about this, Molly shot back silently. Admit it's your obsession with getting an heir and not Raoul's that must be fed. But she was too polite to confront her hostess that way. She doubted if Gabrielle set much store by the truth unless it justified some course of action she wanted to take.

"I realize Siobhan's asking a great deal of one so young who has never borne a child," the older woman continued in the face of her silence. "To carry an infant and give it up...even to one's nearest and dearest...would take a great deal of courage. No one will think badly of you if you refuse."

How generous you are, Molly thought, again biting back the first words that sprang to her lips. She didn't need a ton of bricks to fall on her in order to realize Gabrielle was calling her a coward.

"I'm happy to hear it, Mme de Montfort," she responded, her air composed though her dark eyes flashed with displeasure. "But...even if my sister were to disown me over this...my decision would be the same."

Though she could scarcely be pleased at Molly's opposition to what had become her plan, too, Gabrielle didn't let it show. "Permit me to hope we can change your mind, then," she said evenly. "The child you could give us would be a very great blessing."

Her steamroller-of-calm approach was almost more than Molly could take. Unwittingly she found herself sympathizing with her sister, who had lived under Gabrielle's thumb for more than eleven years. What hell it must be for her sometimes, she thought—even with Raoul for a husband.

"Supposing I *were* to agree," she said abruptly, pushed to the limit of her endurance. "What if the baby turned out to be a girl? It's been known to happen."

This time, there was no mistaking the imperious flash in Gabrielle's eyes. No firstborn grandchild of hers would dare to do such a thing.

Seconds later the emotional shutters were firmly back in place. "Of course we'd treasure any baby of Raoul's," the older woman answered, the bedrock of her equanimity undisturbed.

Closeted in a budget meeting with about twenty other members of the National Assembly, Raoul couldn't seem to keep his mind on France's fiscal affairs. As if they had a will of their own, his thoughts kept returning to the way Molly had looked that morning as she'd rested her hand so lightly against the wall of the Roman bath. In her flat shoes, peach-colored outfit and ponytail, she'd seemed almost like a schoolgirl. But she was a grown woman—sensitive, caring and emotionally complex. His inner man had recognized that all too well.

He hadn't brought Siobhan to his "quiet place" even once during the years of their marriage, guessing she'd laugh at his romantic notions. A self-styled pragmatist, his wife lived strictly in the present moment. Yet she ignored the most pressing reality of all, in his opinion—the fact that life was fleeting and should be lived with the utmost fidelity and grace. From the very beginning, though he hadn't seen it then, she'd been too superficial, too mocking to share his somber moods and more fanciful imaginings.

Molly, on the other hand, had understood immediately what he felt. Like him, she'd listened to the bright silence in that little courtyard and heard the echoes of centuries. So easily that it sent shivers over his skin, her big brown eyes had gazed at the ruin and seen the refuge it offered from the petty tyranny of events.

What would it be like to have a woman like that? he wondered. To be the focus of her affection and goodness, let her generosity permeate your life?

Ask though he might, it was a moot question. He was tied to Siobhan and there would never be a woman like Molly for him. Even so, the thought of how it would feel to have her carry his child in her body—though he would never touch her to plant his seed—twisted like a knife in his gut. I'd want to be beside her every minute, watch the shape of our child grow in her belly and feel the flutter of its movements, he admitted, temporarily abandoning his scruples to emotion. Look on with pleasure and adoration as she nursed it at her breast.

Don't be a fool, he ordered himself in the next breath. None of those things would ever be possible. If Siobhan got her way, *she'd* be the baby's mother, not Molly. You'd be reduced to watching a nanny administer its bottle while your wife was out gadding at some social event.

Yet he couldn't help picturing how a baby that sprung from his and Molly's genes would look. He or she would have dark hair and its mother's beautiful eyes. Willfully he conjured up a miniature version of himself in knee pants, let the image dissolve to one of a small, dimpled enchantress who cried, "Papa!" and held out her arms.

It wouldn't do. Thinking such thoughts would only exacerbate the way he felt.

You're thirty-eight, he reminded himself, struggling to explain his aberrant mental behavior. And though you've long since given up on the idea of children, perhaps there's something buried deep inside you that misses being a father. If so, you can just forget it. You're stuck with Siobhan and she wouldn't give you a child even if she were physically able. As for Molly, she must never be permitted to make such a sacrifice.

Calling back that evening as promised, the Air France ticket agent informed Molly she was holding a place for her on a Paris-to-New York flight in three days' time.

"As you requested, I managed to get a second seat for your traveling companion, Father Fitzwilliam, together with a connecting flight for him from New York to Palm Beach," the woman said.

"Three days!"

Though Molly's exclamation was barely audible, the agent caught it. "I'm truly sorry, madame," she apologized. "But it's the best I could do on such short notice. We could transfer you to another airline and gain almost twenty-four hours but the cost would be prohibitive."

When she learned just *how* prohibitive, Molly decided to make the best of the situation. Relieved that she was standing firm, Matt readily agreed to leave when she did. He even praised her maturity in handling the situation.

With their new reservations, they'd manage to eliminate more than a week of the emotional roller coaster their visit had become. While Matt visits with some friends from his seminary days, I'll stay scarce, tour the city, do some shopping, she thought. I'll simply refuse to discuss the matter again.

She didn't want to admit she was beginning to waver. For one thing, Gabrielle's argument that having a baby for Raoul and Siobhan would be a loving, courageous thing to do had hit its mark whether or not she cared to admit it. Siobhan's woebegone expression and the guilt Molly felt over her own unwilling attraction to her sister's husband were also taking their toll.

But perhaps the most telling factor was the look on Raoul's face. Though she'd expected him to stay away after the morning's blowup with his mother and Siobhan, he'd taken his place that night at the head of the dinner table. His brooding, unhappy air had struck straight to her heart.

If Siobhan would turn over a new leaf and do her best to make him happy, she thought, it might almost be worth the invasion of privacy and potential heartbreak having a baby for them would entail. God knew there was a part of her that *wanted* to do it, for reasons she didn't want to face.

That night, a dream nudged Molly over the brink. In it, she and Raoul were leaning over a wicker bassinet trimmed in white lace and blue ribbons. A baby was napping inside, cuddled beneath a light blue, fuzzy blanket. Lovingly her dream-self noted the perfect shape of its head, its silken dark hair and tiny, delicate fingers. With a start, she realized the child belonged to them.

"He's beautiful," Raoul whispered, taking her in his arms. His hands on her breasts, he began to make love to her while the baby slept. At the mercy of her subconscious, Molly responded with a burst of passion unlike anything she'd ever experienced in real life. A moment later she was sitting up in bed. Her heart was pounding. Beads of perspiration stood out on her forehead.

Dear God! she prayed. Please don't send me such terrible thoughts! But she knew the dream had originated with her, not the Almighty. Its message was clear: she wanted Raoul—not as the twelve-year-old child she'd once been but as a woman.

With a groan, she covered her eyes. I've wronged my sister grievously, if only in my heart, Molly accused herself, sinking back against the pillows. Though she doesn't realize it, I *owe* her whatever assistance I can give in the fight to save her marriage. I'll probably live to regret it. But I'm going to tell her in the morning that I've changed my mind.

She broke the news to Matt over the breakfast table, shortly after he returned from saying Mass. He was horrified.

"Molly, you *can't!*" he exclaimed, his colorless brows elevating at the shock of her pronouncement and a dull red flush spreading upward from his collar. "You don't know what you're saying!"

"Maybe not."

She gave him a rueful look. Though she was half-inclined to agree with him, she felt the die had been cast. Now she just wanted to go ahead with things. She'd wrestled with her conscience long enough.

"I think I have to help her, Matt," she said, knowing she could never explain her real motives to him. "I can't just turn my back and walk away when I'm the only one she can ask."

He shook his head disbelievingly. "I thought you understood. The Church doesn't approve..."

"I realize that. And generally I agree, especially where money is to change hands. But I don't see why it would be wrong in this case. I'd be giving Siobhan...and Raoul...the gift of a child purely out of love. There'd be nothing in it for me."

Nothing but absolution, that is, she added ironically to herself. They were alone in the breakfast room. As if some kind of physical activity had suddenly become essential to his survival, Matt got up and began to pace.

"You're right about one thing at least," he said, turning to face her. "A child *is* a gift...but from God, not man. We only cooperate in the giving, within the bonds of holy matrimony. For us to pervert His design for our convenience is a sin."

"Can you really call it that if one of the marriage partners can't have a child?"

Matt nodded emphatically. "Subjectively good intentions don't change the character of moral law. Of course I feel for Siobhan. And for Raoul. But surrogate motherhood is a far greater evil than childlessness. It reduces an infant to a commodity, perverts the sexuality of the adult participants and attacks the concept of family at its roots."

"I honestly can't see how that's so." Molly broke off a piece of croissant, then decided she didn't have much appetite. "There'd be no 'commodity' in this case because I wouldn't be paid," she said. "You can hardly call artificial insemination sexual by the furthest stretch of the imagination. As for attacking Siobhan's marriage, or her *family*, as you put it, what I'm about to do will save it, not bring it down. There may be a great many valid reasons against what I've decided to do, but I don't think you've hit on any of them."

Molly didn't have to be told that a certain stubbornness, which had surfaced in her character periodically since she was small, was shining from her eyes. She supposed Matt couldn't help but be aware of it. We could argue all day, she told him silently, and it wouldn't change a thing. We're talking on different levels. You're quoting Church teaching. And I'm coming from the heart.

"A child has the right to a direct filial relationship with his parental origins," he said stiffly as if he knew he was losing ground.

"Then why is adoption sanctioned?"

He brushed the question aside. "That's a wholly different matter and you know it. But since you bring it up, why *doesn't* Siobhan adopt? With everything they have to offer, she and Raoul shouldn't have any difficulty getting a child."

Molly hesitated, knowing what her brother's reaction would be. "I think it's because of Gabrielle," she admitted at last. "When it comes to inheriting the title, an adopted child wouldn't make the grade."

Matt rolled his eyes in disgust. But he didn't resurrect his argument about convenience being the worst sort of motivation.

"If you go ahead with this," he warned instead, "it could cause you incalculable damage, both emotionally and physically... maybe even ruin your life. Because I love you, I don't want that to happen. You may as well know it. I plan to call Aunt Rosie and ask her help in changing your mind."

Predictably Siobhan was jubilant. "Oh, baby!" she exclaimed, hugging Molly and waltzing her around an elegant Louis XV salon. "You've made me the happiest woman in the world! I promise ... I'll be the very *best* mother. You'll never be sorry you said yes!''

"I hope not." Though her tone was solemn, Molly had to smile at her sister's exuberance. "I trust you won't forget your other promise to me," she said.

Siobhan's brows shot up as if she couldn't imagine herself doing such a thing. "Me? Be unfaithful to Raoul? *Never!*" she vowed. "I'll write a letter ending things with Marc and have it hand-delivered to him this afternoon. Afterward, we can go out shopping for baby clothes."

"Don't start celebrating yet." Feeling more like a sacrificial lamb by the minute now that she'd given her word, Molly laid a cautionary hand on her sister's arm.

"I don't understand."

"It remains to be seen if I can get pregnant. And Raoul hasn't agreed to cooperate."

Siobhan resumed her merry little jig. "Don't worry," she insisted, "you'll be able to. As for Raoul, I can handle him!"

Aunt Rosie was out when Matt phoned. To his obvious dismay, when she called back, she merely listened, warned Molly of the emotional pitfalls she might encounter and advised her to listen to her heart. Following their three-way conversation, Matt withdrew into a frustrated and worried silence.

By contrast, Raoul went through the roof when Siobhan told him Molly had capitulated. "What did you do to make her give in?" he demanded. "Threaten suicide or something equally ridiculous?"

He refused to believe she'd reconsidered of her own accord. Bitterly he took Siobhan to task for what he called her "utter selfishness and total lack of regard" for her sister's well being.

"I have no intention of taking part in this mad scheme even if Molly's willing," he concluded, his face a furious mask. "Try and get around that if you can, *chèrie!*"

Slamming the door forcefully on his way out, he went in search of his sister-in-law.

A short time earlier, oppressed by the weight of her decision and the tense atmosphere in the house, Molly had sought the relative peace of the garden. Absorbed in her thoughts, she'd wandered some distance along the path, almost to the vine-covered wall that separated the de Montfort property from its neighbor on the next street. Through the trees, she glimpsed the pearl-gray walls of a smaller, far less pretentious structure.

Absently she noted that the pitch of its slate roof and the modified arch of its Palladian windows proclaimed it a gem of late eighteenth-century architecture. If I were ever to live in Paris, she thought, I'd prefer a house like that to the de Montforts' splendid residence. But though she'd be aunt—and godmother, Siobhan insisted—to the child she'd agreed to carry, self-preservation and her unfortunate feelings for that baby's father dictated she cut all emotional ties with them.

If I have a grain of sense, I'll stay away from France during its growing-up years, she told herself. Maybe if I don't learn to love it, rock it to sleep in my arms or rejoice at its first footsteps, giving it up may not leave such a gaping hole in my heart.

If she was lucky, she might even get over Raoul.

She turned at his footsteps on the path. In truth, she'd been bracing herself all day for his reaction. She didn't expect it to be serene.

As she'd guessed it would be, his voice was rough when he spoke. But he didn't appear to be angry with her. His forehead was furrowed with concern and regret as he grasped her hands.

"What happened to make you change your mind?" he asked with an underlying gentleness that touched her heart.

She shrugged. "I thought about things, began to see Siobhan's point of view."

"And that is?"

"A baby will bring the two of you back together. Her happiness...and yours, of course...mean a great deal to me." He would never know how much.

Raoul was silent a moment as they faced each other in the twilight. She was wearing another of her schoolgirl outfits—a short-sleeved white angora pullover, gray glen plaid skirt and pearls. In it, she looked as fresh and appealing as a nosegay of gardenias still wet with dew. Even so, the emotional strain she'd undergone as a result of Siobhan's pleading was clearly visible in her eyes.

"Did my wife...or my mother...exert undue pressure on you?" he asked.

She shook her head. "No more than might have been expected."

"Then this is your own decision, arrived at after careful consideration?"

Molly nodded. Again there was silence.

"I can't let them do this to you," he said, reaching out to brush a stray lock of hair back from her forehead. "Without my cooperation, they won't be able to."

What a beautiful man he is, Molly thought. And so unhappy in his family situation. "Have it your way, then," she replied softly, trying not to let him see how much his tenderness had affected her or guess the depth of her concern for him.

Chapter Four

By morning, Raoul had changed his mind. No one would ever know what fierce archangels of thought he'd wrestled with in the night, or what painful conflicts had tormented him. But though his eyes were haunted still, he'd vanquished them by the time he asked Gabrielle, Siobhan, Molly and Matt to meet with him in the blue-and-gold salon.

"I called everyone together to say that I've withdrawn my opposition to Siobhan," he said, looking first at his wife and then at Gabrielle. "If she and Molly are convinced a surrogate arrangement is what they want, I won't stand in their way."

"Raoul!" Delightedly Siobhan threw her arms about his neck. "Darling, I don't believe it! What made you change your mind?"

His quick glance at Molly was unreadable. "Suffice it to say that I did," he answered. "Contrary to what you seem to believe, I wouldn't find it disagreeable to be a parent."

Had Siobhan lied when she claimed Raoul wanted an heir? Had she blamed their childlessness on him? Molly couldn't subscribe to either possibility. She felt overwhelmed now that the last roadblock to what Siobhan was proposing had been removed. *I wonder what swayed him?* she thought. *I doubt he'll ever tell anyone. I can only hope that, deep down, he still loves Siobhan and wants to make a go of their marriage.*

Declaring herself contented with the way things had worked out, Gabrielle gave Matt a benign look. "I'm aware you opposed this idea when it was first presented to you, Father," she said. "Nonetheless, I hope we can count on your blessing."

Expecting a lengthy argument from Matt, Molly braced herself. His face had darkened like a thundercloud when Raoul had announced his change of heart. But apparently her brother didn't feel there was anything to be gained by conducting theological postmortems.

"I'm afraid I couldn't go that far, Mme de Montfort," he said, his tone dry and humorless. "You are right when you say I'm against what my sisters are planning. However, I won't raise any further objections provided the utmost care is taken to protect Molly's interests."

"Of course they should be protected," the elder *comtesse* agreed at once. "It's only fair. What do you suggest?"

Matt paused. "I'd like to see an agreement drawn up specifying everyone's rights and obligations in this matter."

"Oh, Matt!" Siobhan made a face at him.

"I only want the best for everyone here...even if I don't approve of what you're doing. But Molly has the most to lose in this and she's my first concern. I know we're family. But I still think it would be a good idea to have a contract."

The following afternoon, Raoul, Siobhan, Gabrielle, Molly and Matt visited the de Montforts' family attorney in his legal offices. As they waited in awkward silence, a lengthy legal document was drawn up to Matt's specifications. It provided that Raoul and Siobhan would take full responsibility for any child Molly might carry for them under its terms immediately upon the baby's birth. In return, Molly agreed to relinquish to them the child she might conceive as a result of impregnation with Raoul's semen. Siobhan agreed to adopt the child under French law.

Molly's hand shook as she signed the typewritten pact followed by Raoul and Siobhan, with Gabrielle and Matt acting as witnesses. This is really happening, she thought. I just don't believe it yet.

Apologizing to the Air France agent, she changed their reservations yet again. Five days later, at the optimal time in her menstrual cycle, she was inseminated at a private clinic where Raoul had gone the day before to perform his task as donor. Lying on an examining table with her legs spread apart as if for a routine visit to the gynecologist, she felt terribly vulnerable and alone. She was on the verge of backing out of the whole thing.

But it was already too late. With the insertion of something cold and metallic that produced a brief sensation of pressure, the unfamiliar physician had quickly completed his task. Can conception really take place like this? Molly wondered as a nurse covered her lower body with a sheet. The procedure was so sanitized, so impersonal, more like a lab experiment than an act of procreation. *Is that all there is to it?* she burned to ask.

A tremor passed over her skin when she realized just what had happened.

We've barely touched and yet, if this technique works, in a few months I'll feel Raoul's baby moving inside me, she thought as a chatty, upbeat Siobhan drove her back to the house. Afraid what she was feeling might show in her face, Molly avoided Raoul for the few hours that remained until their departure and said very little to anyone.

They left promptly for the States the next day. Noting her wan look and the emotional strain that was evident in every line of her body as their plane soared high above the Atlantic, Matt shook his head. "I don't care if you *are* a grown woman with the right to make her own mistakes," he raged quietly. "If the insemination didn't take this time, I'm not going to let you go through it again."

Molly's first weeks back in the U.S. were so busy as she attended fashion premieres and negotiated purchases for the shop with designers and manufacturers that she had little time to brood. It was only at the close of each day, when her quotidian round of shows and business meetings was over, that she abandoned herself to melancholy thoughts.

It didn't surprise her that she found it difficult to sleep. In deference to the possible presence of an embryo in her womb, she didn't resort to sleeping pills. She even thought twice about taking two aspirin for a headache. When business contacts or friends from college days invited her out to dine, her ethics didn't permit the use of alcohol.

But though emotionally she was on tenterhooks, she didn't record any physical changes of note. By the time she'd returned to Palm Beach, she'd almost convinced herself the insemination was a failure. Hadn't the French physician who performed it remarked it often took several tries to produce results? Meanwhile nothing in her agreement with Siobhan and Raoul stated she must continue to make herself available until success was achieved. Counting herself lucky to have escaped from her promise so easily, she bought advance supplies for her monthly cycle at a local drugstore.

When her period didn't come, she began to fret. Had the process worked after all? She certainly didn't feel sick. Nor had she experienced even a trace of the morning nausea conventional wisdom had taught her to expect. Instead she was in blooming health, literally bursting with energy and joie de vivre.

Could my period be late because of the emotional stress I've undergone recently? she asked herself. I understand that can sometimes be the case. Now that she was home safe in her everyday life, surrounded by her own concerns and pursuits, she preferred to forget the events that had taken place in Paris more than a month before.

But her body wouldn't let her. Each day that passed without a ripple to discern it from the one before she became more certain that she *was* pregnant.

Finally Aunt Rosie talked her into seeing a doctor. "Hiding from the truth won't make it go away, my dear child," she said, gently patting Molly's hand as if she yearned to offer more tangible support. "If you're going to have a baby, it deserves the very best prenatal care."

Submitting to a brief but thorough exam by her gynecologist, Molly wasn't sure what she wanted the outcome to be. From her point of view, she supposed, it would be far better if the pregnancy turned out to be a false alarm. If that happened, she'd be free, permanently off the hook. Yet she knew without putting the thought into words that some elemental part of herself would be deeply disappointed.

A sheen of gooseflesh spread over her arms when the doctor confirmed she was going to have a child.

"Congratulations, Mrs. Dunlap," he said, giving her a warm, paternalistic smile. "You're about two months pregnant. So far, everything seems to be going well."

Molly hugged herself in the elevator as she returned to the parking area. It was incredible but true: she was going to have Raoul's baby! The miracle of life, which had fascinated her since she was small, was at that very moment unfolding within her like a flower.

In her mingled joy, uncertainty and regret, she wasn't sure whether to cry or cheer. Whatever happens, Raoul and I are irretrievably joined in the tiny scrap of humanity that lives within me, she told herself, knowing she should banish such thinking from her head. Siobhan's handsome, moody husband could never be hers. Yet she couldn't help rejoicing at the chance to give him such a wonderful present. Because of the way she felt about him, she realized, carrying his child would be a bittersweet experience.

Siobhan was ecstatic when Molly phoned her with the news. "I'll never be able to thank you enough for what you've done," she gushed over the satellite connection.

"All I ask is that you get your act together with Raoul," Molly answered. "I trust you've honored our agreement."

"You mean about Marc?" Her sister's voice was steady, reassuring. "I haven't seen him in ages," she said.

"As for Raoul, I think we're getting along a little better. He probably won't admit it. But I suspect he'll be as happy as I am when I tell him the news."

Molly was nearly four months pregnant when she first felt the baby move. She was relaxing in the garden of her aunt's Palm Beach home, gazing out at the sun-dazzled water and remembering the excited lilt in Siobhan's voice when she'd learned she and her husband would become parents.

Suddenly there was a faint fluttering in her stomach, so slight at first that she believed she was imagining things. Then it came again and she realized it was her child, trying out its first independent movements.

Siobhan and Raoul's child, she corrected herself hastily, forcing down the swell of maternal feeling that rose up out of nowhere to claim her heart. You're just the vessel charged with bringing it into the world.

Just then, in the house behind her, the phone rang. Caroline would get it. Molly didn't move in the hope of feeling that faint, precious fluttering again.

To her surprise, a minute later the housekeeper was hurrying toward her across the lawn. An overweight, middle-aged woman, she usually moved with slow, deliberate footsteps. Now she was puffing with exertion and visibly out of breath.

"Miss Molly, it's Father Matt," Caroline said in an anxious voice, halting by Molly's chair. "He says he tried your aunt at the shop but she wasn't in, that he needs to talk to you right away!"

Something of the housekeeper's alarm transferred itself to Molly and she all but flew into the house.

"What *is* it, Matt?" she asked, her heart pounding as she snatched up the receiver. "Caroline seems to think..."

"Brace yourself." Matt's voice was brimming with some terrible emotion. "Maybe you'd better sit down," he added, as if he'd just remembered her physical state.

"All right." Pulling out an antique chair that matched the rolltop desk in her aunt's study, Molly fought to stem a rising tide of panic. "I'm sitting," she said. "Go ahead and tell me.... What's this all about?"

Briefly her brother was silent as if searching for the best way to break an unbearable piece of news. "There's been a terrorist shooting at Roissy-Charles de Gaulle," he said at last. "Siobhan got caught in the cross fire. They don't expect her to make it."

Molly gasped, her free hand covering her mouth. The truth was so horrible, so devastating, she would have fainted on the spot if Matt hadn't ordered her to a seat.

This can't be happening, she protested, her mind struggling with the reality of it. Siobhan's so beautiful, so full of life, so happy at the thought that she and Raoul are finally about to become parents. Even in a world filled with injustice and pain, she *can't* be cut down by a terrorist's bullet!

"Nooooooo!" she screamed in horror, reliving the heartbreaking news of her parents' and Sean's demise so many years before. "Please...tell me this is all a dream!"

"I wish to God I could." Matt's words were a knell, a pitiless reality indoctrination. "Look," he said, "you have to think of the baby. Promise me you won't try to go anywhere or do anything until I get there. Have Caroline fix you a cup of hot tea or something. I have to call the bishop and then I'm heading in your direction.

I've already made reservations for you, me and Aunt Rosie out of Palm Beach shortly before noon.''

Their trip to Paris was grim—a Chinese water torture of waiting as their jet ate up the miles that separated them from the grievously wounded person of Comtesse Siobhan Fitzwilliam de Montfort. With each minute that ticked away, they got a little closer. But each minute that passed could also bring her death.

Her mind flitting from visions of Siobhan's laughing face to imagined scenes of mayhem at the huge international airport where they were now headed, Molly recalled Aunt Rosie bringing home a black silk crepe shift for her from the shop and packing it carefully into her suitcase. With more presence of mind than either Matt or Molly possessed, it seemed, she was anticipating a funeral.

Raoul's face was ashen and there were dark circles under his eyes when he met them at the gate. ''Thank heaven you're here,'' he murmured roughly, embracing each of them in turn.

A few signs of the recent shoot-out were still evident in the main terminal. Her face blank as if the tragedy that had occurred earlier had wiped it clean of all expression, Molly took in her surroundings. Where did it happen? she wondered. There, by the ticket counter? Or over by the magazine stand?

For his part, Raoul couldn't keep his eyes from roving over the shape of Molly's body beneath the gray silk chemise she'd worn for the trip. She was still very slim, he saw. But the gentle swell of her previously flat stomach was unmistakable.

That's my child she's carrying, he thought, longing to put out his hand and touch the curving fullness that testified to the baby's presence. A moment later, he berated himself for his lack of control. For God's sake, what kind of man are you? he asked himself. At this very moment your wife may be dying. And she *is* your wife— even if she hasn't behaved like one in years.

Feeling his eyes on her and guessing the reason, Molly pushed all thought of Raoul from her mind. She was here for Siobhan's sake and for that reason only. She drew her pale gray raincoat around her in an effort to hide her pregnant state.

"How is she?" Matt asked as they made their way through customs.

"Critical." Raoul raked his fingers distractedly through his hair. "She took three bullets," he explained. "One at the base of the skull and two in the stomach. The doctors say it's a miracle she's still alive."

"She has a fighting spirit." The words were Aunt Rosie's and they seemed to offer a slender thread of hope.

Hurriedly they piled into the Citroën and raced to the hospital with Raoul at the wheel. "I'm not sure they'll let you come near her," he warned as he let them off at the front entrance. "There's been talk of more surgery. . . to relieve the pressure on her brain."

While Raoul parked the car, they hurried upstairs to the intensive care unit. Siobhan lay white and still behind a glass partition. A myriad of tubes connected her to IV packs, oxygen, blood and a heart monitor. Though she was still breathing, her chest barely seemed to move. Her cheeks were sunken, her head bandaged. Medical personnel had shorn away most of her glorious auburn hair.

"How is she?" Matt asked again in his awkward French when a nurse came out to them.

"About the same." Switching into English, she gave them a sympathetic look. "The doctor will be checking on her again in just a few minutes, *mon père,*" she added. "I'll make certain you have a chance to speak with him."

"May we ... go inside?"

The nurse glanced at Molly, obviously noting her pregnancy and assessing the state of her nerves. "For just a moment," she said kindly. "If you like, you might tell her you're here. She's in a coma, *vous savez*. But it's my belief comatose patients can hear what's being said to them. Sometimes the presence of family members encourages them to fight."

Her heart breaking at her sister's pitiful condition, Molly lightly stroked Siobhan's hand. "We're here, Sib," she whispered. "You have to pull out of this. The baby..."

Touching the shape of her niece's foot beneath the white hospital sheet, Aunt Rosie didn't say a word. Matt choked out a blessing as tears rolled down his cheeks.

A moment later, Raoul joined them as they walked out into the hall. "You must be tired after your long journey," he said with the sustained weariness of one who has already sat many hours beside a sickbed. "There's a visitors' room this way."

For what seemed like an eternity, the four of them banded together in the small, anonymously furnished room, drinking the hospital's strong, chicory-laden coffee and bracing themselves for periodic bulletins from the doctor. The brief visits they were allowed told what little there was to tell. Siobhan continued to cling tenaciously to life. Yet somehow her spirit seemed to be moving farther and farther away from them.

Finally the physician in charge of her case ducked into the waiting room to tell them he was going off duty. "I don't expect the crisis to come within the next few hours," he said. "Another doctor will keep watch on her. He's fully competent. And I give you my word—the hospital will call you immediately if there's any change. It would be best to take your relatives home for some rest, M de Montfort. Otherwise we'll find ourselves treating them, as well."

Realizing they couldn't keep up a twenty-four-hour-a-day vigil, Molly, Matt and Aunt Rosie agreed to let Raoul drive them to the de Montfort residence.

"What happened?" Matt asked as they traversed the city of dreams, so civilized and timeless with its floodlit necklace of public monuments.

Initially Raoul seemed reluctant to speak. "Siobhan was scheduled on a flight to the Midi," he answered after a moment. "She was checking in her bags when the shooting broke out."

Matt appeared to digest the information. "The Midi...that's the south of France, isn't it?" he asked. "Was she going to the family château?"

"No," Raoul responded shortly.

"Where, then?"

Molly could feel Matt digging in with his typical Fitzwilliam stubbornness.

"As I understand it, the Riviera." Raoul's words were clipped.

"By herself?"

Their brother-in-law's silence was longer this time. "Not exactly," he admitted. "Marc St. Onge, whom I believe you've met, has a condominium there."

A muscle tightened beside his mouth as Molly and her relatives absorbed the news. Forgive me, he begged her silently, keeping his eyes on the road. I didn't want to tell anybody about this. You least of all, after what you've done for us. But I suppose you'd have found out anyway in the normal course of events.

Molly was more distraught than she'd ever been in her life as she climbed into the canopied bed where she'd slept during her previous visit. Siobhan is horribly wounded, she thought. She could die. Yet competing for dominance with Molly's grief and worry was an overwhelming tide of anger and disappointment.

After convincing Molly to bear a child on her behalf, Siobhan had quickly thrown dirt in the face of her promise to end her affair and patch things up with her husband. It appeared that she'd never had the slightest intention of doing any such thing.

Whatever she did, you can't hold a grudge against her now, Molly reminded herself, punching her pillow into shape as she courted sleep. Your every thought must be aimed like an arrow at the target of her recovery. But she couldn't help wondering as the small presence in her womb fluttered again what would become of the child she'd conceived out of love for her sister and guilt over Raoul.

They were up again and on their way back to the hospital by 6:00 a.m. To Molly's distress, they were greeted by a pack of journalists brandishing video cameras, microphones and notebooks.

"M le Député!" one of the reporters shouted as he and his colleagues mobbed Raoul and nearly trampled the rest of the family in their efforts to get to him. "How is your wife, the *comtesse?*"

"Is she going to make it?" screamed another.

"Do you plan to push for more stringent measures against terrorists as a result of this tragedy?" a third demanded.

A mask of calm descending over his features, Raoul the public man gestured at his in-laws to go ahead while he paused to give his answers for the record. With a backward glance, Molly hurried after Matt and Aunt Rosie into the hospital.

If anything, Siobhan seemed to have sunk further into the coma caused by the bullet lodged at the base of her brain. Molly began to wonder if Siobhan would be herself again, even if she pulled through. Raoul appeared a few minutes later, his face slightly drawn from the rough-and-tumble of the interview. He arrived just in time to share the latest bulletin on Siobhan's condition. It wasn't good.

"There's very little we can do now except wait and hope for a miracle," the physician told them frankly, his eyes filled with compassion behind the round spectacles he wore. "She appears to be sinking. But it's certain she wouldn't survive another operation to relieve cranial pressure."

Wrapped in the cotton batting of emotional shock, yet tensing with fear each time a nurse checked her sister's pulse, Molly waited out the last minutes and seconds of Siobhan's life. She was pronounced dead at 10:05 a.m. His face like stone, Raoul signed the necessary papers. Bending to kiss her sister for the last time, Molly wiped away bitter tears.

A few minutes later, they were escorted down the back staircase and into the Citroën, which a hospital employee had brought around so they could avoid the press. Thus sheltered from prying questions, they returned like automatons to the Villa Montmorency.

The day was sunny and mild, a mockery of everything Molly felt as Gabrielle de Montfort met them at the door. One look at their faces and the senior *comtesse* clearly guessed what had transpired.

"I am so sorry, *mes enfants,*" she murmured, astonishing Molly by electing to embrace her first. "Siobhan was too young to die. But perhaps it was a mercy, if her injuries were as terrible as they thought."

A fierce and willful part of Molly wanted to shriek in protest. How dare you write off my sister like that? she raged. Yet in her heart, she knew Gabrielle was right.

Like actors in a set piece of tragedy, they assembled in the salon where Siobhan had waltzed Molly around after she'd agreed to act as a surrogate. Everything was the same, yet incredibly, shockingly different. That morning, as Martine offered coffee and brandy from a silver tray, the elegant furniture resembled a stiff collection of props. The room's heavy brocade curtains were drawn to keep out the glare.

Siobhan would never waltz again, never hold the baby she'd professed to want so much. Meanwhile that small, blindly trusting presence was developing, growing and learning to suck its thumb within Molly's womb. When it was born, it deserved to be received into the arms of two loving parents. Unfortunately, the document they'd drawn up that day in the attorney's office hadn't provided for this kind of catastrophe. What would happen now was anybody's guess.

Chapter Five

Following a formal service in Paris attended by most of Raoul's fellow deputies and their wives, Siobhan was laid to rest in a private ceremony at Château de Montfort, the turreted, sixteenth-century family seat on the River Cher. In the placid, mossy cemetery that held the remains of so many generations of Raoul's family, Molly said a final goodbye to her sister. I don't approve of the way you lived your life, she whispered. But I love you, Sib. And I always will.

She wasn't ready, either emotionally or physically, when Gabrielle summoned everyone to a family conference in a small salon that overlooked the gardens and the river beyond. All too quickly she learned that the topic under discussion was to be her own pregnancy and the ultimate disposition of the baby she'd agreed to bear for Siobhan and Raoul.

"Because of Siobhan's untimely death, we find ourselves in something of a dilemma," Gabrielle noted, searching their faces. "Earlier this morning I spoke with Father Matt about what is to be done now with respect to the child Molly is carrying. We're of the same mind . . ."

Matt looked thunderstruck, as if he feared Gabrielle was about to attribute a boldly unconditional meaning to some provisional statement of his. Raoul was frowning, a wary expression in his eyes. How could you do this to me? Molly demanded silently of her brother. I'm pregnant, not mentally disabled. I don't appreciate you consulting with outsiders about how to dispose of my baby!

But Gabrielle wasn't an outsider; she was the baby's grandmother. And Matt was its uncle. Certain rights attached. The elder *comtesse* made that plain, insisting in the same breath that she and Father Matt cared only for the infant's welfare.

"It's our contention that Raoul and Molly should be married at once for the sake of their child," she concluded. "That way, any gossip that's stirred up will have had a chance to die down before the baby's birth."

"*No!* I absolutely refuse!"

Molly half rose from her chair, her figure still relatively slender in the black shift she was wearing. For her to marry Raoul on the heels of Siobhan's funeral would be unthinkable, a kind of sacrilege. Hidden away deep in her psyche was the irrational fear that somehow she'd caused her sister's terrible fate by coveting the husband Siobhan hadn't seemed to love.

But Molly hadn't wanted to covet him. To be thrust upon him now against his will, in a loveless marriage entered into solely for their baby's sake, would be a far greater punishment than she could bear.

"I . . . never agreed to anything like that when I consented to bear a child for my sister and her husband," Molly added in a shaken voice.

Instantly Raoul entered what had all the earmarks of a family free-for-all on her side. "Molly's right," he said. "It's not fair she should be trapped by her generosity. Naturally I'll honor the agreement my wife and I made with her and accept the child as my heir."

He made it sound as if she didn't want the baby. Unconsciously she rested one hand on her stomach as a strong protective urge swept her body.

"You mean . . . raise it here in France?" she asked incredulously. "Alone?"

Raoul shrugged. "What else can I do? I'm now a widower. I'll be forced to hire a nursemaid. And later a governess. I must admit that the so-called family atmosphere of the de Montfort household leaves a great deal to be desired."

Gabrielle gave her son a forbidding look, then quickly turned to Matt. "Tell your sister what you told me," she said.

Matt looked even more ill at ease. Meanwhile Aunt Rosie hadn't said a word.

"Go ahead . . . tell her," Gabrielle insisted.

"There's not much to tell." Molly's sincere, freckle-faced brother sent her a look that pleaded for understanding. "If you must know, I merely acknowledged that, in God's eyes, the best place for any child is in a stable home, with two loving parents to guide and care for him. But that doesn't mean I'm convinced Molly should wed in haste. There could be drawbacks. I just feel that perhaps she should consider marriage to Raoul as one of her options. . . ."

By now Molly's lower lip was trembling. Tears were threatening to spill from beneath her lashes. Figuratively at least, she and her baby were being tossed about like a football. She wasn't going to stand for it!

"As far as I'm concerned, Siobhan's death canceled any agreement we had," she said, her dark eyes ablaze. "Raoul needn't take on a burden he doesn't want. As the baby's mother, I'll work something out!"

Without giving anyone a chance to reply, she bolted from the room. Fueled by her anger, she walked rapidly down to the château's river landing. She was trembling with fury as she stared at breeze-blown willows and rippling water. The scene that met her eyes was so quiet, so tranquil, it might have been a mirage.

Quickly Matt was by her side. "Are you all right?" he asked.

"Yes, I think so. It seems that, unlike Siobhan, I'm cut out for childbearing."

For the first time in Molly's memory, the emotional distance that separated them was like a canyon, wide and deep.

"I want you to know she twisted what I said all out of proportion," Matt said humbly. "And that I'm sorry I spoke to her about it in the first place. I should have insisted you be in on the conversation."

"It's okay." Forgiving him, Molly leaned her head on Matt's shoulder. "Tell me what you really think," she said.

His mouth twisted in a wry grin. "Promise you won't get angry again."

"I'll try not to."

"Okay. In essence, if not in motive, I think Gabrielle is right."

Though Molly stiffened, she didn't pull away.

"The last thing I want to see you do is commit to a loveless marriage," Matt went on, picking his words with obvious care. "I know you've said you don't plan to get involved with anyone again. But you may change your mind someday. And in the eyes of the Church, you'd be tied to Raoul.

"Still, in this situation, it seems to me, you must put the good of an innocent baby first. If you wish, your union with Raoul need only be a formality. Once your vows are spoken, you can return to your life in the States."

"And our child?"

"I get the impression you'd be more than happy to mother it yourself."

There was a small silence in which Molly considered his point of view. "You're right about that, anyway," she said.

When she asked Aunt Rosie for her opinion later that day in the chaâteau rose garden, Molly was told only that the decision was *hers* to make.

"Of course you must think of the baby, but you shouldn't forget your own welfare in this, either," her aunt reminded. "You're much too prone to do exactly that, dear child."

The two of them had just settled on a pair of stone benches beneath an arbor hung with tender buds and nodding, full-blown roses when Raoul hesitantly joined them.

"I hope I'm not intruding," he said, a somber figure in his mourning clothes. "But Molly and I must talk."

"Indeed you must," Rosie replied, getting to her feet. "Please excuse me. I feel a nap coming on."

Seated across from her as honeybees buzzed in the trellis overhead, Raoul thought how young and vulnerable Molly looked. But though her face was pale with grief, her pregnancy seemed to agree with her. He had never found her more beautiful.

How unfair it would be for her to be saddled with Siobhan's cast-off husband—a man fifteen years older than herself whom she didn't love—simply because of one generous act, he mused. Yet he knew she was under a great deal of pressure, even from Matt, to do as Gabrielle wished. Somehow, he had to find the right words to set her free.

"I want you to know that I fully support your refusal to marry simply for the sake of our child," he told her. "I myself have reasons for declining such an alliance. For one thing, at thirty-eight, I'm much too old for a young woman like yourself. And there are too many unhappy memories between us. I'm sure you're well aware that my union with your sister was far from ideal."

He took a deep breath, then continued, "Though I'll love and nurture the baby you're carrying to the best of my ability if you decide that its place is with me, I'd prefer to forget the anguish of the past. And that won't be possible if I strengthen my ties to your family instead of pulling away."

Molly's eyes widened as if she'd been slapped. It was bad enough for Raoul to talk of her not being imprisoned in a loveless relationship. But to learn he wanted nothing to do with her was like a dagger plunged in her breast. To make matters worse, it seemed he expected her to turn over their baby to him, perhaps never see it again!

"It's settled, then," she answered abruptly, hoping someday to eradicate his handsome, somber visage from her thoughts. "I'll return to Florida with my family the day after tomorrow. As for our child's future, I haven't decided how I feel about that yet. I may choose to raise it myself in Siobhan's absence. Naturally I'll always recognize its status as your heir."

* * *

Word of her decision quickly reached Gabrielle. "It won't do," the senior *comtesse* told Raoul in no uncertain terms after summoning him to her private boudoir. "If Molly chooses to ignore her contract with you, neither the family nor your political career can stand the scandal of a court case. Yet if we allow her to raise your son by herself in America, the next Comte Beaulieu de Montfort will have Yankee manners. He'll lack the aristocratic *French* upbringing necessary for him to assume his rightful place in the world."

Raoul's expression didn't change. "What makes you so sure the baby will be a boy?" he asked.

"I just *know*."

He gave her a sadly amused, ironic look. "Even if you're right, Maman, how can you justify using a defenseless young woman like that to achieve your ends?"

In response, Raoul's mother drew herself up to her full height. "If you cared half as much for the welfare of that 'defenseless young woman' as you'd have me believe, you'd be eager to marry her to safeguard her reputation," she decreed. "As for myself, I claim no such noble sentiments. I admit unflinchingly that I put my grandson's welfare first."

Molly, Matt and Rosie were to leave by private plane for Paris's Le Bourget airport around dinnertime. Deciding the agreed upon timetable could go to hell, Raoul strode down to the stables and saddled his favorite horse. He was gone a long time, riding alone through the low hills and vineyards that had belonged to his ancestors for centuries and on past the boundary of his family's property as far as the breathtakingly lovely *bâtiment* of Chenonceaux. He felt propelled by events outside his control.

Wouldn't it have been wonderful to bring Molly here simply as a friend this afternoon? he thought. I know she'd have found it as beautiful as I do. Like some grim specter of denial, Siobhan's death had stood in the way. Molly was grieving for her sister; she'd never understand why he was unable to, or why he felt a sense of relief at her passing though he'd have given anything to avert the tragedy that had taken place.

Unless he missed his guess, however, it wasn't just that Siobhan was gone or even the awkward fact that Molly was having his baby that kept them at arm's length. From the day of their first meeting, so long ago, something in Molly's attitude had whispered that the door of friendship would be forever closed to them. If for a single moment he dared to think otherwise...

Raoul returned to the château at dusk. The rest of the family was already packed and waiting. Not stopping to speak with anyone, he went upstairs and knocked on Molly's door. A flame of emotion he couldn't define blazed up in her dark eyes when she saw him standing there.

It was quickly hidden. "Come in," she told him.

Taking care not to brush against her, he stepped into the room. "I'll be brief," he began, his voice deep and a little rough. "I've had time to think and I've concluded I was too hasty this afternoon in my assessment of our situation. I now feel Maman and your brother are right...our child needs the security that can only be provided by parents who are formally married to each other. Accordingly, I ask you to be my wife. You may rest assured I won't exact the usual privileges of a husband."

Molly stared at him, completely unable to speak for a moment. A thousand thoughts were racing through her head. "I plan to fly back to the States day after tomorrow," she managed at last.

He nodded. "I don't see why that should interfere."

Slowly she grasped what he seemed to be telling her. She and their child could enjoy the protection of his name, yet she'd be free to live her own life, as before. He wouldn't object if she returned to America. Perhaps he even wanted her to go.

What a fitting punishment this is for coveting my sister's husband, she thought, even though I've struggled against my feelings for him from the very first! Now I can have him. All I have to do is say *yes*. Yet he'll be permanently out of reach.

The truth was, she, too, had been having second thoughts. She had no quarrel with Matt's advice that the baby's welfare should be of prime importance in her decision-making. And maybe that meant she should marry Raoul. She was beginning to think it did. Marriage would banish forever any possible stain of illegitimacy. Meanwhile she'd lost her only ally in refusing—unless she counted Aunt Rosie, who wouldn't say what she really thought.

You, first, little one, she told her unborn child as she looked up into its father's face. Being tied to Raoul, yet remaining scrupulously separate from him, won't be easy. But I chose to bring you into this world for reasons that were complex, to say the very least. And I owe you the best possible start in life.

"All right," she said, letting the tension drain out of her shoulders as she ceased all protest. "I'll marry you if you think that's what we ought to do."

They were joined the following afternoon in the library of the de Montforts' Paris house by special dispensation of the usual waiting period. It was a somber occasion. Everyone wore black, as if they were still attending a funeral. Only their immediate family members were present. Though Molly had asked Matt to officiate, he'd demurred, relegating the honor to the local parish priest.

Molly knew without having to be told that Gabrielle was deeply satisfied at getting her own way. She sensed Aunt Rosie still had reservations. Matt seemed relieved but unhappy. Like Rosie, she guessed, he was concerned that she'd given up any chance of a future with the man of her choice. Little did they suspect how she really felt. Only Marie-Claude, with her malicious, knowing gaze, made Molly feel as if the woman could read her mind.

Though her voice was steady as she repeated her vows, Molly's hand shook when Raoul slipped his ring on her finger. I'm his *wife*, she thought. Can fate really be this devious? Siobhan had been dead only a few days. Yet the scent, the touch of him when he bent down to brush her lips with a nuptial kiss was so intoxicating she wanted to swoon in his arms.

At dinner that night, conversation was strained. Though the plain gold band put there by Raoul had replaced Kirk's diamond wedding set on the third finger of her left hand, Molly still couldn't believe they were married, let alone the fact that she was a countess in her sister's stead. Picking at the exquisitely prepared *côtelettes d'agneau* on her plate, she raised herself from lethargy as Gabrielle spoke.

In her quietly tyrannical way, Raoul's mother was speaking of the excellent French obstetricians available. Apparently she believed that when Matt Fitzwilliam and Rosie O'Meara returned to America, Molly would remain behind.

"Pardon me, but I already *have* an excellent obstetrician near my home in Palm Beach," she told her new mother-in-law. "Since I'll be returning there tomorrow, I see no reason to change doctors."

Immediately following the meal, Molly closeted herself in the guest room she'd previously occupied. One of the maids had brought her Siobhan's jewels, furs and other personal objects to sort through and decide which she wanted to sell, which to keep. It was a painful task, one that constantly reduced her to tears.

Oh, Sib, she thought with grief. What would you say if you knew what's been going on? Much as I love Raoul, I would never have wanted you to die, never have hoped to be married to him in your place. A life of exile would be far better, if you were alive and happy with him. But even as she wept and dabbed at her eyes, the rational part of her insisted Siobhan and Raoul had never been happy.

Meanwhile her new husband had once again been summoned into his mother's presence.

"Your wife announced at the dinner table that she's planning to go back to Florida tomorrow," Gabrielle told him. "It mustn't be allowed to happen."

Raoul stared at her. "Just what do you expect me to do about it?" he asked. "Restrain her physically? Or fall on my knees and beg her to remain here, with a man she didn't want and doesn't love?"

His mother gave him a contemptuous look. "If pleas are too humble for your taste, then you must do your duty as a husband," she said. "In a word, the marriage must be consummated. Otherwise it will be much too simple for her to get an annulment, thus plunging us into the very difficulties we hoped to avoid."

Though he knew his mother well, Raoul was shocked at the extent of her determination. "You mean . . . force myself on Siobhan's grieving sister?'' he asked in disbelief.

"I mean *make love to her*," Gabrielle answered. "You're a Frenchman, aren't you? You *do* remember how?"

Just as she'd done when Siobhan had first proposed her surrogate-mother scheme to Gabrielle, Marie-Claude was listening outside the door. She crept away, clearly delighted with her new tidbit of information.

If Gabrielle de Montfort weren't his mother, Raoul believed, he'd have slapped her face. But he'd never struck a woman and he didn't plan to start.

"I'd never submit Molly to that kind of indignity to please you or anyone," he told Gabrielle shortly, turning his back on her and leaving the room.

He shut himself up in his study and poured a stiff drink. Downing it in one gulp, he fixed himself another. What Maman was asking him to do was outrageous, an insult to his manhood not to mention Molly's virtue. He'd see the woman who had given him life in hell before he'd take orders of that sort!

Gradually the edge of his fury blunted though he was still angry enough to wring his mother's neck. I need to warn Molly, he thought. If Maman can't use me, she'll find some other means of getting what she wants.

Finishing off a third drink, he started up the stairs. Outside Molly's room, he heard the soft sound of weeping. His hand on the knob, he opened the door a crack. On a chaise lounge were scattered several piles of personal items belonging to his late wife. The woman he'd just married that afternoon was crying as she looked through a picture album.

As he watched, she wiped her eyes, closed the album and set it aside. A moment later she was turning out the lamp. In the moonlight that bathed the room, the outline of her body was visible through the pale, thin nightgown she wore. He could clearly see the dark smudges of her nipples, the precious bulge of her abdomen that contained his child.

"Oh, Siobhan," she murmured, thinking herself alone as fresh tears slid down her cheeks. "Why did you have to die and leave things in such a mess?"

The alcohol buzzing in his head, Raoul wanted nothing more than to comfort her. "Molly?" he asked, pushing the door open a little wider.

"Oh, Raoul..."

On her lips his name was an entreaty, one he couldn't resist. Stepping inside, he closed the door and took her in his arms. At first he simply sheltered her against him, absorbing her tears into his shirt and tenderly stroking the satiny sweep of dark hair that fell forward over her face.

Except for their brief encounter on the dance floor of the Northland Country Club when she was twelve, it was the first time he'd ever held her. He could feel the swell of her pregnancy, the delicate ridge of her backbone, her lush, engorging breasts.

Maman was right about one thing though she didn't put it into so many words, he thought. It's been a long time since I've made love. But then he'd never had a wife like Molly. Never one who was carrying his child.

Almost before he realized what was happening, he had tightened his embrace. Her softness was so entrancing, so wantonly delicious he couldn't get enough of it. Simultaneously rapacious and protective feelings that hadn't stirred in his blood for years were rapidly getting out of control.

Nestling against the hard wall of Raoul's chest, Molly could feel his heartbeat as if it were her own. Though the guilt feelings spurred by his relationship to Siobhan and her sister's tragic death ran deep, she wanted to burst with joy at the chance to touch him that way. How am I going to stand it, she asked herself, being married to the one man in the world that I want, yet knowing all he feels for me is gratitude, compassion and a brother-in-law's regard? Yet even those crumbs of affection could sustain her, she believed, if offered freely by Raoul's hands.

"Molly... *jeune femme précieuse*..."

Abandoning the use of English with his scruples, Raoul buried his face in her neck. The scent of her hair was like apple blossoms in the springtime. Through the thin silk of her gown, his strong, capable hands explored the shape of her body the way a blind man's would. The brush of his mouth against her skin formed itself into kisses filled with desperation.

Completely stunned by the unexpected turn things had taken, Molly clung to him as to a life preserver. She was drowning in need and only he could save her. Even as their child fluttered in her belly, an answering stab of desire more potent than anything she'd ever experienced pierced her to the core.

"Please, Raoul... take me," she heard herself whisper as she gave way to the heedless abandon of the moment.

"Ah, Molly... I've always wanted you so much!"

With the admission, which had slipped from him in the heat of passion, Raoul swept her up in his arms. Fifteen years and the memory of a dead woman separated them. Uniting them were the pounding of their separate pulses in unison, the deep and forbidden attraction that had always caused their eyes to meet, then refocus elsewhere, seeking refuge from the treacherous magnet-pull of desire.

Lovingly he carried her to the bed and laid her back against the pillows. Her eyes were languorous, her hair in disarray, her lips parted as if in expectation of his mouth.

"Will you really let me have you?" he asked, slowly unbuttoning his shirt.

His bare chest—broad, well muscled and covered with a tangled mat of crisp, dark hair—was so beautiful it made her heart ache. With all the yearning she was capable of, she wanted him inside her.

"Yes . . . oh, yes, Raoul!" she breathed, slipping partway into his language as if it could better express what she felt. "*J'ai besoin de ton corps, ton âme . . .* whatever you can give. . . ."

She wanted his body, his soul. The last remnants of Raoul's control crumbled at her frank admission. Stepping out of his trousers and removing his shorts, he gently eased the straps of her gown from her shoulders.

"The baby," she whispered.

He deposited a kiss on one corner of her mouth and then the other. "I won't hurt you, *chérie.*"

"It isn't that."

"What, then?" Lightly his fingertips traced her breasts and teased the miniature volcanoes of their peaks.

"I don't have . . . a waist anymore. I might not please you."

A stab of longing—so intense he'd never felt its equal—coursed through him. "Don't you know," he asked incredulously, "that you're lovely beyond compare?"

There was no further need for words. Taking off her gown the rest of the way, Raoul abandoned himself to loving worship. To Molly's ineffable delight, he feathered lingering kisses on the swell of her stomach and exacted sweet torment from her swollen, aching buds.

In a kaleidoscope of seconds, it seemed, they'd gone from uneasy separateness to this: a world as self-contained as a lotus flower with themselves the only inhabitants. *I don't know how he feels, but Raoul is all I'll ever need,* Molly thought as she opened her mouth to his. *No one else could overwhelm me this way if I lived a million years.*

The gentleman in him, the considerate lover, wanted to make it last. But he had needed her for an eternity. With great tenderness and care he hovered over her, matching her length for length.

Now I've tasted heaven, Raoul thought. She was so giving as she cradled him in the depths of her womanhood, tilting her lower body up to meet his, that it brought tears to his eyes. He wanted to lay everything he had, everything he was at her feet.

For a moment he held them motionless as he recovered himself, girding his impatience for their ascent. But neither of them could wait for long. That night, with moonlight washing their tangled bodies and the sweet scent of their lovemaking hanging on the air like perfume, he brought Molly to her very first shattering climax. Up and up she soared, with each plateau more excruciatingly delicious, more helplessly profound than the last, until finally she broke free in an exaltation of shudders that rocked her very soul.

They were one—as intimately joined, as perfectly welded as if they shared the same skin. The world seemed to have rearranged itself on its axis as they drifted down together.

"Were we wrong?" Molly asked when finally she could speak again.

One of Raoul's long, muscular legs was still wrapped protectively around her. As she gloried in its weight, her head rested comfortably on his shoulder. She felt as if a tremendous electrical charge had swept her body, leaving it supple, spent, at peace.

"To make love the way we did?"

Remembering his mother's outrageous dictum, he felt a moment of shame. But it didn't arise out of what they'd just done. I didn't consummate our marriage out of obedience to Maman but in answer to the urging of my heart, he thought. Once we'd breached the barrier of our isolation, not to make love to each other would have been like trying to stop an avalanche.

"No, we weren't wrong," he said at last. "We each need very badly what the other can give."

Curved about each other like spoons, with his hand on her stomach so that he could feel the movement of their child, they fell asleep.

In the morning, Raoul was gone. For a moment Molly panicked, thinking he regretted what had happened after all. Then she realized their changed situation still wasn't generally known in the household. It would be a delicate task to break the news of how they felt about each other. Knowing Raoul as she did, she guessed he'd want to be tactful—particularly in view of the situation.

It would be up to her to square things with Matt and Aunt Rosie, find a reason to delay her departure. With thoughts of how to do that racing through her head, and a precarious trust in what the future would bring filling her heart, she dressed and went downstairs. For once, Gabrielle wasn't holding court in the breakfast room. Instead, Marie-Claude was its sole occupant. She gave

Molly a malicious, almost triumphant look as she larded butter onto her brioche.

"I see my brother hasn't lost his touch," she remarked in answer to Molly's tentative *"Bon jour."*

Molly frowned. "I don't know what you mean."

"Oh, I think you do." The smile on Raoul's sister's face would have done credit to the Cheshire cat. "You have the delicate blush, the sated look of a woman who has been thoroughly and passionately used. Of course you must have guessed the reason for Raoul's timely performance."

This time, Molly said nothing. She held her breath.

"I was outside Maman's dressing room last night," Marie-Claude continued, taking an oversize bite of her brioche and dabbing at a thin stream of butter that ran down her chin. "I heard her order him to make love to you so you couldn't get an annulment once you'd returned to the United States."

Chapter Six

Molly's disillusionment was terrible and swift. It was suddenly, painfully clear that Raoul hadn't really wanted her. The sweet, open-mouthed kisses he'd placed on her belly and breasts had been nothing more than a lie. Ditto his magnificent lovemaking that had carried her to the gates of paradise. In the most profound sense, she realized, he hadn't made love to her at all. Instead, he'd only been using her. She felt infinitely worse knowing he'd done so at his mother's request.

All she had left was her pride. Summoning its strength to be her armor, she refused to let Marie-Claude see her weep. Never mind that she felt betrayed, stripped naked, spat upon by the man she loved. I've got to get out of here, she thought, envisioning herself as a small, gray mouse caught in a trap. I can't ever let this happen again.

It took every ounce of nerve she possessed to murmur something civil about not being hungry after all and quietly leave the room. Alone in the hall she began to shake as if she had a chill. Surely this is a nightmare, she told herself. But she knew it wasn't. Racing up the stairs, she began feverishly packing her things.

In an exclusive jewelry shop on the swank Boulevard Montmorency, Raoul was choosing a ruby ring set in gold for Molly's finger. When he returned, he planned on asking her to marry him all over again.

I want the ring that symbolizes our true joining to resonate with the color of passion rather than the cold, impersonal glitter of diamonds, he thought, half beside himself.

Writing out his personal check to cover the ruby's exorbitant cost, he pocketed its tiny velvet presentation box and left the store at a half run. By now Molly would be awake and wondering what had become of him. He was as eager as a boy to rush to her side, explain what was in his heart before the moment's uncertainty swept her away.

For some reason, thanks to the unexpected kindness of the gods or a benign whim of fate, he'd been given a second chance at happiness. Molly Fitzwilliam Dunlap, now Molly de Montfort, with her fresh view of the world and her trusting, generous nature, was now his wife. She was carrying his child within her body. The future opened out before him like a flower in time-lapse photography—full, translucent, tremulous with the dew of fulfillment. His only charge was to treasure her, let her know in whatever words or gestures he could muster just how precious she was.

Naturally, given Siobhan's recent death, they'd have to be discreet. A certain amount of time would have to pass before even the family could be let in on their secret. Still, in essence, his marriage to Molly's sister had been over for years. Morally he and Molly were well within their rights.

So thinking, Raoul parked the Citroën on the cobbled court in front of his house and hurried inside. Taking the stairs two at a time, he went straight to Molly's room. To his amazement, the bed had been stripped of the linens they'd shared. She was dressed for travel, putting the last of her things away and closing her cases.

"What's going on?" he asked, feeling as if he'd been kicked in the stomach.

You needn't continue your act on my behalf, Molly thought. *I* know. "Our plane leaves at twenty past twelve," she answered without looking at him. "Surely you remember."

He stared at her, uncomprehending. "Of course," he acknowledged. "But I thought . . ."

"That after last night, I'd stay?"

Abruptly her brown eyes met his hazel ones, blazingly direct. Yet it was a frosty fire that they contained. The chill penetrated to the very marrow of his bones. *Yes,* he answered her silently. *At least that's what I had hoped. I thought we'd found something wonderful together.*

"What we did last night was wrong." Molly spoke as if her pronouncement was as irrefutable as the laws of physics. "My mistake as well as yours," she went on when he didn't answer her. "Marie-Claude told me about your mother's insistence our marriage be consummated. I'm afraid my excuse was a bit flimsier...the simple need for comfort in my grief. What happened, happened. Now it's time to forget."

Molly's renewed emotional distance and his sister's unprovoked treachery cut Raoul like a knife. *You should have known better than to expect something so beautiful to grow out of your barren and ruinous marriage to*

Siobhan, he thought. But even if Molly was determined to leave him, he didn't want her to go believing he'd made love to her on Gabrielle's orders. Was it possible she'd listen to the truth?

Think a moment, he ordered himself. She's already told you in so many words that what you assumed from the beginning is correct: her feelings for you aren't those of a wife or lover. All she wanted from you was a moment's forgetfulness—brief, physical and not to be repeated. You really *would* be forcing yourself on her if you undermined her reasons to go.

"At least let me drive you to the airport," he said, his hands clenching at his sides and the ring box a forgotten lump in his pocket.

"That won't be necessary." As she glanced at him again, Molly's face was closed, a slate wiped clean of any hope that they could communicate. "Your manservant has been kind enough to call us a cab."

Raoul had already left the house by the time she, Matt and Aunt Rosie departed. As their plane took off from the same airport where Siobhan had been struck down less than a week before and circled over one of the world's most beautiful and cosmopolitan cities, Molly wondered if she'd ever see Paris again.

The child she was carrying would grow to love it, of course. Part of the baby's future lay there, with the man who had cooperated in giving him or her life— bequeathing, perhaps, his rapier-swift intelligence, extraordinary eyes and brooding mouth.

For her part, Molly wasn't sure she'd ever be able to bear visiting Paris again. In her mind it would always be inseparable from Raoul. And, despite the cool facade she'd presented to him that morning, her heart was aching for him. The truth was she loved him more than ever, though her respect for him had diminished. He didn't bother to deny Marie-Claude's accusations, she thought—not even to salvage my self-esteem!

"Feeling okay?" Matt reached over to pat her hand while, on Molly's other side, Aunt Rosie took out her knitting.

"Physically, yes." Suddenly more tired than she'd ever been in her life, Molly leaned her head against his shoulder. "I still can't believe Siobhan's gone."

"Neither can I." Her brother was silent a moment, a faraway look in his eyes. "With the deaths of our parents, Sean, and now Sib, our family has sustained more than its share of tragedy," he added. "At first I was against your bearing this child for Siobhan. But now I'm glad you overruled me. In a very special way, we still have something of her with us. Your baby would never have been conceived if she hadn't given birth to the idea first."

For Raoul, the months of Molly's pregnancy slowly passed. As his unborn infant grew toward the maturity of birth an ocean apart from him, Raoul was busy in the French National Assembly, concentrating on more stringent anti-terrorism measures.

Only at night, when sleep wouldn't come, did he allow Molly to creep into his mind. Alone in his room he imagined the lust-provoking scent of her bare skin against his nostrils and the forthright seriousness that shone from her big brown eyes. He began to think nothing would ever erase the imprint their lovemaking had made on him. The rest of his days, it seemed, would be measured by her absence, even if he lived to be very old.

Molly's health continued to glow into her seventh month and beyond. Yet her child grew steadily heavier.

Realizing motherhood could take its toll, she dropped back to a part-time schedule at the shop and sometimes napped in the afternoons. For the baby's sake, she tried to put Raoul out of her mind and embrace a vegetative state.

Though the husband she refused to acknowledge as such called from France every week to check on her and ask if there was anything she needed, she didn't often speak with him herself. Stung by her obvious reluctance to indulge in even that limited form of communication with him, he'd apparently learned it was better to phone in the evenings, when Aunt Rosie would be home to take his call.

Yet though she'd rigorously outlined a separate life for herself, Molly continued to long for Raoul's touch. Again and again her thoughts returned to the night they'd spent together. How could anyone seem so passionate, so tender, yet simply be following orders to commit a conjugal act? she wondered. The baby was kicking all the time now, and she yearned to have him place his hand on her stomach and feel its movement, just as he had when they'd fallen asleep in each other's arms.

Molly's delivery date was a month away when Raoul found an excuse for business travel to the States. An international conference on terrorism was being held in Washington, and he'd been invited to speak. First he'd go to Florida and check on Molly himself, he vowed. If she gave him any kind of welcome, he'd remain in the U.S. to see her through the birth.

Molly awakened with an odd sensation pervading her body. She wasn't ill exactly. Things just weren't right.

By noon, she was experiencing regular stomach cramps. Her lunch—half a chicken sandwich, some cottage cheese, fruit and a glass of milk—was quickly re-gurgitated. Beginning to worry, she called Aunt Rosie at the shop and then Matt at his Ft. Lauderdale rectory.

"I have no experience to base it on, but I think the baby's coming early," she said.

Each of them dropped what they were doing and hur-ried to her side.

Raoul arrived at Rosie O'Meara's large, Mediterra-nean-style residence on Lake Worth to find that nobody was home but a man clipping oleander bushes and the housekeeper, Caroline.

"Mr. de Montfort... Oh, my goodness!" the stout, middle-aged woman exclaimed as if he'd materialized out of thin air. "I can't believe you've come at this very mo-ment! The baby's on its way to be born! They just took Miss Molly away to the hospital!"

Pangs of guilt and helplessness rocked him at the thought that she'd gone into labor. The pain she was suffering was his fault!

Quickly he got himself under control. Extracting the hospital's name, address and some rudimentary direc-tions from the housekeeper, Raoul borrowed Molly's car and raced after her. At first, the nurse on the obstetrical floor wouldn't allow him inside the unit. However, when she saw his distraught expression and learned he was the baby's father, she gave way with a smile.

"Raoul!" Matt exclaimed in astonishment from his place beside Molly in the labor room.

"He's...*here*?" Struggling to a sitting position, Molly stared incredulously at the man she loved.

"Yes, if you'll have me," Raoul whispered.

Just the thought of his presence was like a rock and she was desperate to cling to him. Wordlessly she held out her hand.

Their fingers laced together and the rhythm of his breathing buoying hers, Raoul supplanted Matt by Molly's side. Soothing and encouraging her as he wiped the sweat from her brow, he remained close to her throughout the lengthy and somewhat difficult labor and delivery. Tears filled his eyes and he held her hand tightly as she pushed the healthy baby boy they'd created together out into the world.

Squalling lustily from the shock of being born, the baby soon quieted. As his parents watched, he was cleaned up and returned to them in a fuzzy blue blanket much like the one she'd once imagined in a dream. He had a dark head of hair, rosy cheeks and long, dark lashes. One look at him and Molly didn't see how she could ever have dreamed of giving him up—not even to her sister.

I made a questionable decision for noble reasons and, though I wish Siobhan had lived, I'm glad that now I'll be able to keep my son, she thought. Matt was right. In a way Siobhan did leave a life behind.

"World, meet the new Vicomte Beaulieu de Montfort," she said with a lump in her throat.

Raoul was filled with wonder at the baby's tiny, perfect features, his exquisitely formed hands. When he spoke, his voice, too, was husky with emotion. "That's an awfully big name for such a little man," he remarked. "What are we going to call him?"

For a moment they were like any other proud new parents, considering a matter of practical necessity.

"I'd like to name him Sean, after my brother who died in the car accident," Molly said.

Reaching out to his son, Raoul smiled as his finger was grasped by a miniature fist. "How about Sean-Michel?" he asked. "Michel was my grandfather's name."

* * *

By the time Molly and Sean-Michel came home from the hospital, Raoul had made a place for himself in their lives. Without once questioning his welcome, he'd installed himself in Rosie O'Meara's tile-roofed guest cottage. He'd visited them twice a day at the hospital, staying as long and sometimes longer than regulations allowed. And he'd filled Molly's room with roses—so many of them that she felt like some luminary of stage and screen.

Perhaps it was only gratitude that motivated his actions. Or perhaps he was learning to care for her. She didn't dare aim that high, even in the face of his attentiveness and tender looks. Yet a truce had come into being at their son's birth and anything was possible. Following her release, they spent many joy-filled hours together, playing with Sean-Michel.

She knew without being told that Raoul particularly liked to watch the baby nurse. Shy at first about exposing her breast, she decided to be magnanimous. Sean-Michel was his child, too, and she knew it gave him great pleasure to see the baby fed and nurtured. If his honey-colored gaze lingered a bit too long on the lush curve of her bosom, it couldn't be helped. Nor could she be responsible if the sexual tenor of his interest caused little flurries of need to arise in her deepest places—flurries that were only intensified by her son's hungry demand.

Perhaps she was imagining their new rapport. But Molly began to hope against hope itself that someday she and Raoul would be man and wife in a more meaningful sense. She even allowed herself to entertain the idea of living with him in Paris, for part of the year at least. He and their son needed to be close during the boy's growing-up years.

Each time she considered it, the same roadblock stood in her way. She knew she could never live in the same house with Gabrielle and Marie-Claude. To do so would be to subject herself to the tyranny and spiteful tale-carrying that had made her so miserable before. If she was to uproot herself from Palm Beach and begin a whole new life half a world away, she had to find some way to safeguard her independence.

For Raoul the moments he spent with his wife and son represented an idyllic interlude snatched from the swift passage of time. He could hardly bear for it to end. Yet in a few short days he was scheduled to fly to Washington and give his speech. Afterward, the press of obligations would force him to depart for Paris. If only he could convince Molly to bring Sean-Michel and return with him.

Finally, on the day before he was to leave them, he hesitantly broached the subject. To his surprise, she didn't refuse him point-blank.

"I've been thinking about it," she admitted as they walked together beneath a breeze-blown fringe of coconut palms that overhung the water. "A son shouldn't be separated from his father. If you don't mind, I'd like to ask you a question."

"Ask me anything," Raoul replied, keeping hope on a tight leash as his imagination raced ahead of her.

"When we were in France for Siobhan's funeral, I saw a For Sale sign on the house across the garden from yours . . . the eighteenth-century one with the lovely windows. Is it still available?"

Her question seemed a complete non-sequitur. "Yes, I believe it is," he said. "But I don't see . . ."

"Supposing I were to return to Paris with you . . ." Molly began. "Under the circumstances I'd naturally want to maintain my own establishment. If you'll buy that house for me and guarantee Sean-Michel's support, I'll agree to reside there with him for at least three-quarters of every year.''

For a moment, Raoul was speechless. Was it him or his mother and Marie-Claude she wished to keep at arm's length? Perhaps all three of us, he thought. And I wouldn't blame her. But it would be heaven to have her and our son so close.

''I pray the house is still on the market when I return,'' he told her softly, smoothing the baby's cheek. ''Because if it is, I shall most certainly buy it for you.''

Two months later, Molly flew to Paris with her baby and Annie Glynn, the nursemaid she'd hired for him. From their initial meeting, Molly had taken to her new employee. In contrast to her gentle manner with Sean-Michel, the girl had a confident way with adults. Molly believed she'd be loyal while resisting any attempts at intimidation by Gabrielle de Montfort.

Will my arrangement with Raoul work out the way I've planned? Molly wondered as each mile brought her closer to her tall, infinitely masculine husband. Or will temptation strike again, pushing us into bed together?

Ruthlessly she reminded herself that their ''mistake'' hadn't been due to passion on Raoul's part. Though he'd been very good to her since Sean-Michel's birth, she guessed he wouldn't want a too-close relationship. As he'd remarked when he'd first dismissed their marriage as a bad idea, getting involved with her might lead to unhappy memories for him. All his love is for Sean-Michel, she decided. That will have to be enough.

Raoul's eyes were shining when he met their plane. Something more than a simple welcome leaped in their depths as they roved over Molly's once more shapely figure in the slim, rose-colored pique jacket-dress she wore. He was drawn like a magnet to the baby, too.

"Our little man is so big already!" he exclaimed, taking his son in his arms. "If you'd stayed in America much longer I'd have been forced to insist he stop growing until I could actually watch it happen!"

The baby gurgled as if he understood.

Burying his face against his son's warm and tender neck, Raoul thought how much he loved the boy. By some miracle, this adorable, perfect child was flesh of his flesh—the seed of his loins and the fruit of Molly's. He'd never cease to be amazed that she'd actually brought the baby to Paris, where he could watch over them both.

A moment later he relinquished Sean-Michel to Annie's care. Casually resting one hand on the small of Molly's back, he shepherded them through customs and helped them into the family limousine. Molly had ridden in the big, sleek car only once before, on the day of Siobhan's memorial service. Though she did nothing to reciprocate, she didn't shrug off Raoul's touch or move to put more distance between them once they were settled in the limo's plush interior.

Paris greeted her like an old friend—one from whom she'd been estranged in her thoughts. Though the city hadn't changed, she and Raoul had. Incredible as it might seem, *she*, not her sister, was his wife now. The unknown future she'd created by her willingness to risk still lay ahead.

Almost before she knew it, they were turning into the leafy environs of the Villa Montmorency. Jules, the chauffeur, appeared to be headed for the de Montfort family residence. Molly and her husband were friends now for their baby's sake. But friendship had its limits. She wasn't ready to see the house—or Gabrielle—yet.

"I wasn't sure whether you'd want to be installed in your new home right away or spend the night with us," Raoul began, picking up on the resistance she felt. "I had Martine prepare several guest rooms just in case. Fortunately we were able to acquire the Rue Pierre property partly furnished and the beds are made up there, too. It's been thoroughly cleaned and everything is in working order. However, it's not as elegant and comfortable as I might wish..."

Realizing he was rambling, he fell silent.

No way do I intend to sleep under Gabrielle's roof, Molly thought. And that goes double for the room where Raoul and I made love. Though he hadn't said as much, she guessed his mother had probably balked at the idea of her having a separate household.

"The new place, I think," she told him, striving to make her choice seem a casual one. "Sean-Michel, Annie and I will manage there quite nicely. Did I mention that your friend Theo Spassky wrote and offered to help me whip the place into shape? I didn't realize he was a successful interior decorator."

The Rue Pierre house was everything she'd hoped. Pulling up to its entrance for the first time, she had the most extraordinary feeling of coming home. Unlike the de Montfort establishment with its sweeping size and imposing three-story facade, her new abode was petite, understated and welcoming.

Its double front doors, painted a satiny black and flanked by coachman-style lanterns, rose in an arch beneath what she recalled was a "broken" pediment. In good neoclassical style, the floor-to-ceiling windows of the *rez-de-chaussée* were topped by plain horizontal lintels. However, the smaller upstairs windows culminated in slightly flattened arches, echoing the entryway's theme.

By accident Molly's hand brushed against Raoul's as he fitted an oversize key into the lock. Her awareness of him thus sharply enhanced, she couldn't help but think how lovely it would be if he'd carry her over the threshold.

He did the next best thing. While Annie amused the baby, and Aristide, the de Montfort butler, brought over Sean-Michel's new crib, he took her on a tour of the premises. Unlike the great mansion across the garden, Molly's new home had no ornate gilt-trimmed , no marble entry hall. Its rooms echoed half-empty, boasting as they did only a sparse, somewhat drab assortment of the previous owner's furnishings.

She saw the good bones beneath the skin. Personally she didn't care for too much decoration, too many curlicues. And in the absence of enough furniture, she could choose her own.

Those things that truly mattered to her were already in place. The atmosphere was light and airy, the various fireplace mantels uncluttered and serene, the windows as spectacular as she remembered. Crazy about the floors— a mellow *parquet de Versailles* that had acquired a rich patina over the years—she was equally delighted to discover a nursery tucked in between the bedroom she would use and the one she'd relegate to Sean-Michel's nurse.

"Raoul...it's beautiful!" she said softly as they completed their inspection. "Thank you so much for buying this house for us."

"It was my pleasure, *chérie*."

A brief silence ensued and she thought he might lower his mouth to hers. But he didn't.

"Perhaps I should go and let you get some rest," he suggested instead. "Our cook has stocked the kitchen with a few basic provisions. Tomorrow at ten, the owner of a local domestic agency has promised to call. I felt certain you'd want to choose your own staff."

She nodded, considering their mutual recognition of the fact that Gabrielle wouldn't be above planting spies in her household. Reluctantly she saw him to the door.

"Sleep well," he told her, thinking how pleased he was to have her there and how sorry that he couldn't stay. "I'll stop by tomorrow to see Sean-Michel if that's all right. Should you need anything, don't hesitate to call."

Determinedly Molly surveyed her new domain after he'd gone. No second thoughts, she ordered herself. You won't have time for them. Eventually you'll get used to having Raoul so near, yet forever beyond your reach.

She was very thankful for the income bequeathed to her by her parents and the partnership she still owned in Aunt Rosie's shop. Except for Sean-Michel's maintenance, she wouldn't have to depend on her husband's family for anything. Yet she couldn't help thinking of the lonely hours that lay ahead. With Raoul so near—just across the garden—she fully expected to find herself aching for the shelter of his arms.

Several days later, Molly had just hired a housekeeper/cook and a part-time handyman/gardener when Martine arrived with a note from Gabrielle. "Now that you've had time to settle in," her mother-in-law had written in French, "it would be appropriate for you to bring my grandson for a visit. I'll be at home this afternoon."

The invitation was little more than a thinly disguised command, especially since Raoul had taken the baby to see his mother several times. Determined not to wind up under Gabrielle's thumb, Molly fired back a missive of her own. "Perhaps, since I'm now the Comtesse de Montfort and mother of the future count," she scribbled in English, "it would be more appropriate for you to visit me here." To her surprise, the strong-willed and usually unbending Gabrielle complied.

Molly didn't waste any time getting the house in order with Theo Spassky's expert advice and help. On closer acquaintance, Raoul's best friend turned out to be a lovable teddy bear of a man. They quickly became friends.

Theo's entrée to the various shops around Paris that sold rugs, antique furniture and the like proved a godsend. She spent many hours in his company choosing whimsical rococo mirrors, simple white draperies and cushy sofas, armchairs upholstered in rose-colored suede. Their "prize of the hunt" was a rare kilim rug in softly faded colors. Molly placed it to good effect in what she insisted on calling the "living room."

As their work progressed, the little gem of a house took on an ambiance more and more unlike that of Gabrielle's coldly formal establishment. One evening when he dropped by to visit Sean-Michel, Raoul remarked on the difference.

"This place feels more like a home every day," he said half-enviously as he held the baby on his knee.

Molly flushed with pleasure at the compliment. "You might say that's what I've been aiming for," she answered, retrieving their son for his evening meal.

Can it be Raoul might want to live here someday with us? she wondered as she gave the baby her breast. Or will he always be just a visitor? Lovely as this house will be when it's finished, it would represent a step down for him.

For them to share an address and a life wasn't possible anyway as things stood. Marie-Claude's mocking words were too fresh in Molly's ears for that. There was also the small fact that what Raoul felt for her wasn't love.

She didn't plan to settle for gratitude. Meanwhile the garden wall that delineated her property from his was fast becoming something more than ivy-covered stone. Before her eyes it was evolving into a symbol of everything that separated them.

Damn you, Molly de Montfort, she raged after he'd gone home to the mansion beyond the trees. With your foolish passion for Raoul and your Fitzwilliam stubbornness, you've created an impossible situation for yourself.

Chapter Seven

When Sean-Michel was a vigorous five months old, it was time for his formal baptism. Raoul asked Theo to be his son's godfather. Matt, and Aunt Rosie, who had agreed to be the baby's godmother, flew over from Palm Beach for the event.

Charmed despite her egalitarian principles that her son would be the latest in a long line of French aristocrats, Molly searched the boutiques of Paris for the perfect christening dress. Determined to put her own stamp on the occasion, she declined to use the one Gabrielle offered her. Molly's choice—made of tucked linen and hand-worked bobbin lace—was an antique of Flemish origin.

Like his father and grandfather before him, Sean-Michel was to be baptized at an ancient village church near Château de Montfort.

"He looks like a bishop in it!" Raoul chuckled fondly as she dressed their son for the ceremony in his long linen-and-lace garment. "All he needs is a miter and crosier."

He didn't comment on what Molly was wearing. But that didn't mean it had escaped his attention. It was high summer in the Loire Valley, with roses clambering in the hedgerows, and she looked like a rose herself in her deep pink dress. Its flattering cut, which managed to be both demure and sexy, emphasized her lush bosom and tiny waist, the long shapely legs he admired so much.

How different all this might be, he thought as they went downstairs, if I weren't fifteen years Molly's senior and hadn't met her sister first. Yet he knew each human soul, each miracle of conception, was unique. As Sean-Michel's godparents-to-be, uncle and grandmother exclaimed over how handsome the baby looked in his finery, Raoul realized any child he and Molly might have conceived in love instead of a laboratory would have been a completely different person. Though he'd have loved that baby, too, he couldn't imagine a world that wasn't made more joyous by the sweet smiles and bright intelligence of his beloved little boy.

The service, held beside the moldering stone church's baptismal font, was traditional but brief. Sean-Michel cried only once, when the holy water was poured over his forehead. If the priest remembered Molly as the previous countess's pregnant sister and Raoul as Siobhan's grieving husband, he didn't say anything. Neither did anyone else, though such recollections were undoubtedly in all their thoughts.

While they were still at the château, they learned via the evening news that the terrorist responsible for Siobhan's death had been taken into custody. Everyone expressed their profound relief. Yet the announcement brought back many unhappy memories. Raoul reacted to the news by becoming closed and distant. When Molly finally gathered enough courage to ask him how he felt, he shrugged and replied that at last her sister could rest. She felt his answer was only half the story.

Immediately after their return to Paris, Matt flew on to Rome to take part in a special retreat while Aunt Rosie stayed behind to spend a few weeks with Molly and the baby. The shop wouldn't suffer in her absence, she insisted, because a promising young assistant had been hired in Molly's place. Besides, July was always a slow month.

Thinking about the shop made Molly wish she could go back to work again. The house was nearly finished and, with Annie's help in caring for the baby, there wasn't enough to do. She found herself spending a great deal of time daydreaming over Raoul and wondering if her move to Paris had been a mistake. One evening when Theo stopped by, she mentioned her restlessness.

"Why don't you and Rosie open a Paris branch of her Palm Beach boutique?" he suggested. "American chic is always in style."

The idea was so simple and appealing Molly wanted to whoop with delight. Aunt Rosie liked it, too. Why hadn't they thought of it themselves? When Theo mentioned he might be interested in going into business with them, the die was cast. The three of them immediately put their heads together and mapped out a plan.

Though they budgeted carefully, money wasn't a big problem for any of them. A week later, Theo's casual remark had blossomed into a lease for space near his decorating *atelier* off the Rue Jacob and expanded contracts with some of their regular suppliers. Throughout the brainstorming stages, Raoul was only marginally consulted. He felt like the odd man out when he happened on one of their three-way planning sessions.

Molly and Rosie got together for a "mother-daughter" chat the night before the latter's departure.

"*Rosie O'Meara's-Paris* is your baby now," her aunt remarked as they lounged on the embroidered coverlet of the guest room's canopied bed. "I have my hands full back home, so its success will be up to you. However, the work will do you good. And you're more than capable of running things. I'm sure our new brainchild will be a success."

Listening between the lines, Molly detected a note of concern. "What's bothering you, then?" she asked.

In response, Rosie appeared to choose her words with care. "I can't help but wonder what kind of relationship you have with your baby's father," she said at last. "In Palm Beach after Sean-Michel's birth, I thought the two of you might find the makings of a real marriage together. Now it's as if there's a chasm opening between you. Or perhaps you're building a wall. Living in separate houses..."

Her aunt's frank assessment of the situation hit Molly where it hurt. "You know very well, Aunt Rosie," she protested, "that the only way I can safeguard my own identity is to maintain a separate establishment from Gabrielle's."

"Why not ask Raoul to live with you, then?"

Molly had posed the same question to herself a hundred times. For a moment, the deep love she felt for her husband shone forth in her eyes.

"Don't you think I'd like that better than anything on the face of this earth?" she admitted a trifle defensively. "But it would be the wrong thing to do. Just before we were married, Raoul told me he didn't want to remain too closely tied to Siobhan's family because it might bring back memories. He didn't say whether the memories he had in mind were bad ones or good ones. I'm not sure I'd want to know the truth.''

Several days after Rosie had flown home to America, Raoul left on an extended trip to his *département*. He was scheduled to be gone for more than two weeks. Though Molly had originally planned to bring the baby and spend some time with him at the château, she changed her mind at the last minute. She had too much to do, she told him, getting the shop ready for its grand opening.

During his absence, Theo asked her to attend a party with him. At first, she was reluctant, citing her responsibilities to Sean-Michel and the chance that Raoul might disapprove.

"You've done nothing but plan, work and stay at home since you arrived in Paris," Theo argued. "Annie is more than capable of looking after the baby. And I'm between women just now. I need your company. How can Raoul possibly object if you spend an evening with one of his closest friends who also happens to be your business partner...particularly since the two of you lead separate lives?"

He's right, Molly thought with an ache in her heart. Even if it hurts to hear us described that way. Suddenly seeing herself as a pathetic country mouse living on crumbs in the big city, she accepted, though she had the uneasy feeling it was a mistake.

Selecting a smashing and somewhat unorthodox dress from the first batch of arrivals she'd ordered for the shop, Molly graced Theo's arm at the home of the Marquise de Belancourt, one of his wealthiest clients. In her décolleté white gown that sported Western-style fringe and glinted with silver studs, she was much admired. Despite Raoul's absence she actually had a good time until she excused herself to go to the powder room. There, while she was inside the water closet, she heard two women talking—about her husband.

"Louise was devastated when he married so soon after his first wife's death," one of them said. "But then he had to, you know. His second bride was pregnant."

"Louise d'Arignac, setting her cap for Raoul de Montfort?" the other asked. "But why? She has a fine-looking husband . . ."

" . . . who happens to prefer young men."

There was a cluck of understanding. "I think the handsome *député*'s in love with his wife," the other said.

As they left the powder room, the first woman's remark drifted back to where Molly was listening unobserved. "You mean the one who died, of course," she said knowingly. "The Comtesse Siobhan was more his type. . . ."

Heartsick, Molly returned to Theo's side. For his sake, she tried to pretend nothing had happened. But the effort was too much for her. Whispering that she felt ill, she volunteered to call a cab.

"Please don't even suggest such a thing." Theo put one arm around her just as a society photographer snapped their picture. "Of course I'll drive you home."

After telling Theo good-night at her front door, Molly went straight to bed. But she couldn't sleep. I guess I have an answer to the question I posed when Aunt Rosie was here, she thought—if I choose to believe those women. Yet how can I be jealous of my dead sister? Of course Raoul must have loved her or he wouldn't have married her. Losing her was probably very painful for him, even though they'd grown apart.

* * *

Though Raoul doubted that Molly had seen the picture of herself and Theo in print, Marie-Claude certainly had. Ever spiteful, she placed a copy in Raoul's hands when he returned home unexpectedly ahead of schedule. For him, seeing it was like déjà vu. Somehow he'd never believed Molly would carry on affairs the way her sister had. Yet she'd insisted on maintaining separate residences. And though they were united in their love for their son, their marriage was a mere formality. Tormented by the thought that she might be falling in love with his friend, he strode through the garden toward her house.

Theo had come by that very afternoon to consult with Molly on decorating plans for the new shop. At her invitation, he'd remained to sample her housekeeper's excellent cooking. Lonely for the man she loved, Molly was glad of the company. She and Theo were deep in conversation about drapery fabrics and types of carpeting as they sipped after-dinner drinks in her living room when Raoul appeared.

His tawny eyes narrowed at the tableau they made. "I'd like to see the baby," he said.

Molly's cheeks burned though she had nothing to feel guilty about. "When did you get back?" she asked in astonishment. "I thought..."

"This afternoon." Raoul's voice was clipped. "May I see Sean-Michel?"

Embarrassed in front of Theo by his obvious jealousy and stubbornly repeated demand, Molly felt her hackles rise. "He's napping," she responded shortly. "You're welcome to stay for his 11:00 p.m. feeding if you like."

Theo's obviously a favored guest while I'm here on sufferance, Raoul thought, his face tight with displeasure. He's my age. What does he have that I don't?

Clearly sensing an argument in the making, Theo bade them an abrupt good-night.

"Do you realize how unpleasant you've been from the moment you walked in the door?" Molly demanded as Raoul settled in an overstuffed armchair to brood. "You managed to chase Theo away before he could finish his drink."

"Did I indeed?" He sounded more pleased than regretful at the dubious accomplishment. "Perhaps I have no right to ask, but I'm going to anyway," he continued after a long pause. "Is Theo Spassky your lover?"

Molly's eyes widened at the implied accusation. "You're right...it *is* none of your business!" she shot back furiously. She was blazing like a Roman candle at his sudden fit of possessiveness. How dared he behave that way if he didn't want her for himself! "I don't ask you what you do when I'm not around," she added, deliberately fanning the flames.

Raoul's scowl deepened. The almost unbearable tension he felt was visible in every line of his body. "Maybe I'm old-fashioned," he said, "but I won't have you entertaining men with Sean-Michel in the house...even if you have the good taste to choose my best friend as your paramour!"

Totally innocent of any wrongdoing, even in her thoughts, Molly wasn't about to tell him so. They hadn't discussed a morals clause when they'd agreed to marry. She didn't owe him any explanations.

"What about you?" she retorted, wanting to strike where it would wound him the most. "Is it all right if I entertain *you* in my home with the baby upstairs in his crib?"

At her words, Raoul was on his feet. Catching her by the wrist, he drew her tightly against him. She could feel the force of his ire and—heaven help her—his strong arousal. Before she could speak, his mouth was crushing hers, his tongue invading the privacy of her moist recesses. Pent up for so long, the passion he'd taught her during a single night of lovemaking burst free and devoured her protest.

This was what she longed for each night when she lay in bed and thought of him, the secret delirium that haunted her dreams. She wanted his kiss to go on forever—for them to sink to their knees and then to the carpet as they stripped the clothing from each other's bodies. With all her heart, she was aching to make love to him. She wanted him to drown her in sweet forgetting.

It didn't happen. A ragged gasp escaped her as he drew back, leaving her trembling with need.

"Yes, *I'm* an acceptable visitor," he said, his voice taut with the sarcasm she remembered him using to bait her sister. "Like it or not, Mme de Montfort, I'm Sean-Michel's father. And your *husband*. If your sexual desires become too pressing and demand an outlet, you have only to let me know."

Stunned at his blatant cruelty, Molly didn't trust herself to answer as he turned and walked out the door. Oh yes, she thought, heat still quivering in her body. I know only too well how good you are at having sex on demand!

As she nursed her son before going to bed, Molly wondered whether she could stand it if things got any worse between them. She was sorely tempted to give up her new home and all her plans for the new shop and return to America.

Here I am, she thought, accused of infidelity when he's the only man I'll ever want. Yet in his view I can't possibly compare with the woman he once loved, a woman for whose sins I'm now answering.

She had little doubt Raoul would take her again to stake his claim if she gave him the slightest encouragement. But she didn't want him that way. To make love with him now even if it's what I need most would be an exercise in futility, she told herself. I'd ache for him more, not less—the way I did after our wedding night. Yet his basic indifference toward me would remain unchanged.

The day after their confrontation, Molly decided to throw all her energy into her work, at least when she wasn't caring for Sean-Michel. If she could manage to exhaust herself, she reasoned, she wouldn't spend half the night thinking of Raoul and fighting back tears.

Gradually *Rosie O'Meara's-Paris* began to take shape. Even as it did, Molly sensed a new pattern emerging in her life. Following their argument, Raoul almost never visited his son when she was home. Instead, he chose to stop by when the boy was left in Annie's charge. If that's how he wants it, that's fine with me, Molly kidded herself, her Irish temper still close to the boiling point. I don't need Raoul de Montfort to make me happy!

Having shunned Molly while his anger was still hot, Raoul wasn't quite sure how to resume their relationship once it had finally cooled. With a little time to think, he realized shamefacedly that his accusations were probably groundless.

Even if they weren't, he told himself as the pendulum of his emotions swung to the opposite extreme, what happened wasn't Molly's fault. She married me for Sean-Michel's sake—no other reason. She didn't guarantee to love me or be faithful, any more than I made that kind of promise to her. The fact that he'd been celibate since their wedding night didn't enter into it.

It had been raining most of the day one dreary Sunday. Comtesse Gabrielle and Marie-Claude were away, visiting a cousin in Senlis, and the big house on the Avenue de Tilleuls was empty of human companionship. Not that they're ever much company for me, Raoul thought. Semiconvinced he should talk things out with Molly, he threw on a raincoat and walked through the wet garden to her house. But she wasn't at home.

When he questioned Annie concerning her whereabouts, the nursemaid seemed reluctant to answer him. "I believe she and a friend went over to the shop to do some papering," she said at last.

On impulse Raoul decided to visit the shop, as well. He wasn't too surprised when the friend who was helping Molly turned out to be Theo. But he didn't evince any jealousy to his wife's surprise. Noncommittal in her greeting, she returned immediately to her task, leaving Theo to make conversation.

Outside, the rain continued to fall, beading like teardrops on the shop windows and partly obscuring the gray afternoon. Molly and Theo had brought an American-style portable stereo along, and a classical tape was softly playing. A picnic basket stood ready at the foot of a curving staircase.

The atmosphere was casual but cozy, a *mise en scène* that excluded him. Instead of drawing another hasty conclusion, however, he watched and listened, unable to wrest his eyes from Molly's slender figure as she went about her work. She was wearing jeans and an old shirt, and her hair was pulled back in a ponytail. She almost looked like a teenager again as she brushed paste on a long section of paper with fierce concentration.

Drawing Raoul aside, Theo offered him a glass of the wine they'd brought. "She's really something, isn't she, *mon ami?*" he remarked. "So energetic and determined to do something with her life. What a contrast to her sister, who existed only for an endless round of shopping and parties."

His face thoughtful, Raoul didn't answer.

"Look," Theo added when he didn't speak, "I probably shouldn't have said anything about Molly or Siobhan. Forgive me if I was speaking out of turn."

In Raoul's opinion, Theo had been more than tactful and infinitely forbearing of his bad humor. What he saw in his friend's eyes was admiration and liking for his young wife, not concupiscence. He rested a hand on Theo's arm.

"No, you're right," he said as he watched Molly loop the length of paper she'd just pasted over itself and climb with it up a stepladder. Her bottom in the formfitting jeans was so alluring he wanted to reach out and touch it. "Molly's a very special woman," he added. "Siobhan couldn't hold a candle to her."

After his first visit to the shop, Raoul joined in the decorating efforts there—not making any attempt to mastermind them but simply volunteering as an extra pair of hands. All the pensive gentleness Molly liked about him so much returned as if it had never been absent. None of the bitterness and mistrust that had so shocked her was evident.

An idea took hold in her head and she went so far as to make some advance preparations for carrying it out. Yet she wondered if her contemplated bravado was premature. We're getting along better now, she thought, and this could screw everything up—maybe even permanently. But we could go on this way forever if neither of us is willing to take a chance.

Hinting that his mother and a number of his colleagues from the National Assembly—plus their wives, of course—might like to receive invitations, Raoul offered to help host a private soirée introducing Molly's shop to the city's most important clientele on the eve of its grand opening. Both Molly and Theo loved the idea. So did Aunt Rosie when Molly phoned her with the news.

"Something tells me the situation between you and Raoul is improving," her aunt speculated.

Molly laughed, excited over the upswing in her career and more than a little edgy about her secret plan. "Could be," she said evasively. "I'll let you know what develops."

The party, an evening affair to which she'd also invited newspaper columnists and representatives of French, English and American fashion publications, was a great success. Even Gabrielle seemed impressed by her new daughter-in-law's ingenuity and flair.

I *love* being in business again, Molly thought, sparkling as she flitted through the crowd in a red silk slip of a garment. If only my personal life would arrange itself so magnificently. Yet she made one observation that soothed her soul. Louise d'Arignac and her husband, Paul, arrived and chatted for some time with Raoul. Though the lovely, blond Louise might have wished it otherwise, there was nothing for her in Raoul's eyes but the polite conviviality of a good host.

When the last guest had gone, Raoul and Theo helped Molly supervise the catering crew's cleanup effort. Finally it was time to turn out the lights.

"May I see you home?" Raoul asked, tentatively holding out her matching red peau de soie coat.

"Yes, I'd like that," she replied, picking up something new and subtle in his tone. "So will Sean-Michel. He'll want to be fed so you'll have a chance to cuddle him. With all your work here during the past few weeks, you haven't had much time for the baby."

Together, as if they were truly man and wife, they said good-night to Theo and got into Raoul's car. It seemed right and almost comfortable that they should bypass the Avenue de Tilleuls where he lived and enter the Rue Pierre as a couple. A moment later, they were pulling up at her door.

Not quite touching, they walked inside and started up the stairs.

"I'm back.... You can go to sleep now, Annie," Molly called through the partly open door that connected the baby's room to his nursemaid's quarters. "I'll take Sean-Michel to his crib in my room for the night."

It was the first time Raoul had been invited into Molly's bedroom, though he'd seen her nurse their child many times. Breathless with excitement and trying not to show it, he kissed the boy's cheek and then settled in a pale pink armchair facing Molly's beside the unlit hearth. A stab of something that was part lust and part tenderness knifed through him as she lowered one side of her bodice and offered the baby her breast.

Aware of his eyes on her, Molly didn't dare look up. Instead she crooned softly to the baby, humming an old song she remembered from her childhood. But her thoughts weren't really on Sean-Michel. Instead she was remembering for perhaps the hundredth time Raoul's words on the night he'd returned from his *département* and found her conferring with his best friend.

If your sexual needs... demand an outlet, he'd lashed out at her, *you have only to let me know.* Perhaps he didn't mean it, she thought. And I realize he doesn't love me. But it would be heaven to lie in his arms again—even for one night.

When Sean-Michel finished nursing, Raoul held and rocked him for a few minutes before settling him in his crib. A contented if energetic child, Sean-Michel promptly stuffed his thumb in his mouth and closed his eyes.

Reluctantly turning away, Raoul almost bumped into Molly, who had been standing right behind him. *"Pardon,"* he said softly. "I suppose I'd better go."

I want him, Molly thought as she continued to block Raoul's path. So much that it's like an ache pervading my every thought. Why should I stand on pride and deny my heart's fondest wish?

"Were you... serious about what you said the other night?" she asked in a trembling voice.

"On the subject of?"

Like her, he was being excessively careful not to do or say anything that would be detrimental to their relationship.

"Making love to me." The phrase almost caught in Molly's throat.

Raoul was overwhelmed by a powerful rush of feeling. Light-headed and half beside himself with need, he grasped her shoulders. "Can you mean it?" he asked in disbelief. "You're really asking me to stay?"

Chapter Eight

Yes was written all over her face. Her breath whispered it. Her lips invited him. And her eyes! From beneath dark lashes, Molly's big, brown eyes mirrored back his need. The pain of their isolation from each other vanishing, Raoul gathered her into his arms.

She felt so tender, so warm, so unbelievably delicious there. How could he tell her *no?*

"By all that's holy I meant every word," he admitted, his voice muffled against the aromatic silk of her hair. "But not in the rough, unfeeling way I said it. *Ah, chérie...* I wish I'd known what you were thinking tonight. I don't have protection."

"I do," Molly confessed in an embarrassed tone. "I hope it's the right kind. I never bought anything like that before."

Her sweet, resourceful innocence was almost more than he could bear. Molly *planned* this because she wanted me, he thought. Freed of the one contingency that could have prevented him from making love to her, Raoul felt himself grow heavy with desire.

He still had questions. But he didn't expect any answers. From experience he knew she was principled—and possessed a physical drive to rival his own. Like his, her craving for release had long been frustrated. Yet she wasn't the sort of woman to go to bed with anybody but her husband.

Maybe that's all it is, he acknowledged. Simple need. If so, he wasn't too proud to fill it. He'd take whatever she was willing to give.

Something in her eyes offered him hope of more. Could it be that the fifteen-year age difference between them wasn't so important? And that a marriage of convenience could become a marriage of love? If so, perhaps someday they'd be able to lay the past to rest. They were lovers again and, for now, nothing else mattered. Reverently he slipped the thin straps of her red silk gown from her shoulders.

Molly swayed a little as his lean, capable fingers moved on to the placket of her low-backed dress. In a single, fluid motion he lowered the zipper tab. Supple as a second skin, the sexy and utterly feminine creation she'd chosen to excite his interest fell to her feet.

Beneath it she'd worn nothing but see-through lace panties, a matching garter belt and nude-colored hose. Her breasts, visible to him only in glimpses when she nursed their child, were bare as ripe fruit. Meanwhile he still had on his dinner jacket, pleated white shirt and evening trousers, though he'd loosened his formal bow tie. The incongruity of it fired her imagination.

Apparently Raoul enjoyed the contrast, too. Though he shrugged off the jacket and tossed it on the rose-and-white ribbon-patterned carpeting beside her dress, he didn't remove his other garments. Instead he caressed her breasts then bent to unfasten her garter belt and peel down her hose. Her panties followed in seconds. She was besieged with unspeakable delight as his hands roamed her body, worshiping the silk of her skin and seeking the essence of her womanhood. She moaned softly with mounting pleasure and desire.

Her inexperience—the fumblings of a brief, unhappy marriage and one night of splendor in Raoul's arms— made her discovery that much more astonishing. It was possible to burn out of control while still standing on one's feet! Wrapping her arms around her husband, she let him play her like a Stradivarius. Each note, each stroke of the bow brought her that much closer to consummation.

In the flutter of an eyelash, she was crying out with ecstasy. The warmth that had heightened and focused at their most intimate point of contact had exploded in little shudders that racked her body. Swept away by their intensity, she might have fallen if he hadn't steadied her. Chills of rapture raced over her skin.

The flush of her cheeks, radiant with the heat of attainment, told him everything he needed to know. But he wouldn't let her stop there. Each time she thought he was finished, he coaxed her to more. She'd never known such bliss.

When finally she'd had all she could take, he eased her back on the bed. Her dark hair spread out like a halo on the white lace pillows. Still drugged with pleasure, she reached for him.

"In a moment, *mon amour*," he said.

His eyes roving the perfection of her body, Raoul slowly took off his clothes. She was a goddess, spent from the sweet torment evoked by her mortal lover.

Meanwhile, *he* was aching, with the need to make complete love to her. He wanted to bring her back to readiness first.

Molly wasn't deceived. She guessed he was still thinking of her satisfaction. Opening her eyes a little more, she studied him. In the darkened guest room at Gabrielle's house, she hadn't been able to see him well. Here in her boudoir all the lights were blazing. A little tongue of need curled back to life inside her as she took in his broad shoulders, lean hips and his long, muscular legs.

"Come to bed and make love with me," she urged.

Her plea was impossible to resist. His body muscular and heavy on hers, yet taut as a boy's, Raoul came into her arms. Achingly he held her, nearly undone by the texture of her skin and the satiny way it flowed over her lush curves and tender hollows. He was equally intoxicated with her scent, that mysterious blending of soap, expensive cologne and arousal, which combined to create her sexual perfume.

He'd waited for her a long time and he'd planned to savor every moment. But when she began to caress him the way he'd caressed her, it was more than he could handle. Forced to admit his need, he asked hoarsely for the foil packet she'd promised him.

Molly had hidden it under her pillow. Quickly availing himself of its contents, Raoul returned to her embrace and gently began fulfilling their mutual desire.

For a moment he held them motionless. Just the sensation of being part of him threatened to set her off again, and she knew he felt the same. She wanted more—the slow, exquisite climb, the deepening, his face inches above hers as they traded kisses with their eyes.

"C'est bien?" he asked.

"Oh, yes . . . it's wonderful!" she cried softly.

The rhythm began, demanding and inexorable, as slow as they could make it but intensifying still. They were joined like dancers, moving in unison to the drumbeat of their imagination and spontaneous cues phrased in the language of touch. At the center of her being, warmth coiled and expanded. She offered him everything, the very essence of who she was.

Her culmination was implosive and vast, as deep and boundless as creation. Blunt and more powerful than before, huge waves of gratification broke over her. She felt carried out of herself, connected to him and the universe.

Gradually they quieted, embers floating to earth, slowly extinguishing themselves in great oceans of contentment, fields that had known the plow. He shifted his position a little and kissed her neck. She laughed because it tickled. Suddenly they were hugging each other so hard it seemed their bones must break.

A small sound—less than a whimper—emanated from the nearby crib where their son was asleep. Raoul rolled off her and drew her head against his shoulder.

"You know, I think I like making love with the baby in the room," he said. "It makes me feel like a family man."

Though for the moment they'd had enough, they didn't drift off to sleep. That night, Raoul made hungry, passionate love to her again and again. Molly didn't have any way of knowing if that was his usual way with a woman. She only knew it was the way she wanted to be with him. Willingly they pleasured each other again and again.

At last they were too sated to do anything but curl up in each other's arms and turn off the lamps.

"Will you let me stay the night with you?" Raoul asked, remembering it wasn't his house though he felt more at home there now than he did in the great mansion across the garden.

Floating on a sea of bliss, Molly didn't answer for a moment. There haven't been any words of love between us, she thought, despite the conflagration our bodies can make. Maybe we should take things slow. But she couldn't deny she wanted to sleep with him, too.

"As long as you leave before it's light," she answered, hating herself for driving even that small wedge between them. "I don't want anyone else to know about our new arrangement yet."

Molly was still asleep, curled in a ball on her side, when Raoul dressed and checked on their son. His evening clothes rumpled from spending the night on the floor, he stole away just as dawn was breaking over Paris, a reluctant but contented man.

When Molly awoke she reached instinctively for him. Realizing he was gone, she stretched and regretted her cautious answer. Yet nothing could dispel the delicious sense of well-being she felt. It permeated every inch of her body, right down to her toes.

She didn't have time to appreciate her satisfied state. Or even to worry too much if Raoul had been put off by her refusal to let him spend an entire night. She had to feed her son, dress and race off in her new little Renault to the shop's public opening.

When she arrived a few minutes late, Mimi, the dark-skinned, French-speaking woman of Moroccan descent she'd hired as her second-in-command, had everything under control. Business seemed to be picking up already. Glancing about, Molly noticed a huge bouquet of long-stemmed red roses that hadn't been there the night before. The accompanying note was from Raoul. "No color but red is passionate enough to do you justice," he'd written, signing his name in a bold, masculine scrawl.

How I love him! she thought, burying her face among the petals. Even if what he feels for me is only need, it will be enough. To her relief, he seemed to have accepted the new terms of their relationship. And, she had a feeling he'd return to make love to her in the rose-and-white bedroom she shared most nights with Sean-Michel.

During the weeks that followed, Raoul visited that bedroom many times. Yet Molly didn't relax her rule about him leaving before morning came. Though she wished with all her heart she could forget it, Gabrielle's dictum that he make love to her on their wedding night was still a factor in her thinking. So were the remarks Raoul himself had made immediately after Siobhan's funeral. With every appearance of sincerity, he'd agreed with her contention that their marriage shouldn't take place.

It was also a fact that, though he was an impassioned and tender lover, the word *love* had never passed his lips. Was she merely a convenience to him, a way of satisfying his physical needs? she wondered. Or was he carrying a torch for Siobhan? If it was the latter, she couldn't hold it against him. For Molly, her beautiful, exciting sister's memory hadn't faded. How could she blame him if he felt the same?

Raoul was dealing with uncertainties, and he knew Molly must be doing the same. Was he once more taking advantage of her generosity—capitalizing on the fact that she was a very moral young woman trapped in a marriage of convenience with him? Yet despite all the caveats he insisted on flinging at himself, he continued to hope. Surely the delicious heat of her response wasn't totally impersonal.

Nearly every night, they were together. During the daytime hours, Molly found work more satisfying because it left little time for doubts. Empowered by the physical elation she felt, Molly ran the shop like a whirlwind, even designing some of the newest merchandise herself. Legal maneuverings in the case of the terrorist who had murdered Siobhan occupied a good deal of Raoul's attention.

During all that time, Molly refused to make love in Raoul's bed. If they consummated their union in Gabrielle's house, she insisted, everyone would know of it. She still wanted to keep things secret for a little while.

Finally one afternoon when Gabrielle and Marie-Claude left to attend a formal reception in another part of the city, Molly's teasing, persistent husband proposed an assignation in his room.

"Aristide will know," she said. "And Martine. They'll tell your mother."

"I'll give them the afternoon off," he suggested.

"Oh, no!" Her eyes sparkled at the thought of it. "That really *would* amount to a confession!"

Ultimately she gave in, acceding to her own wishes as well as his. Feeling like a wicked schoolgirl and all the more aroused because of it, she sneaked upstairs with him to his darkly furnished masculine suite of bedroom, dressing room and bath. His bed was huge, a four-poster in dark mahogany. Its blankets and sheets, loomed of the finest white wool and cotton, bore a noble-looking monogram.

The effect was a bit intimidating. Giving her a suggestive smile, Raoul produced a tape player of his own. Instead of classical music, he switched on a French pop selection. The song was lusty, sensual, a paraphrase of the act of love.

Unbuttoning his shirt and removing her sweater, he unhooked Molly's bra and invited her to dance. The idea was so outrageous and attractive that pleasure wrenched through her, forestalling any objection.

Her breasts tantalized by the texture of her husband's chest hair, and their lower bodies wedged tightly together, they swayed to the music between bureau and ottoman, dresser and bed. The song's half-whispered words and its marked downbeat were like an aphrodisiac. She found herself pleading with him to make love.

"Here in my bed?" he asked in mock horror, his beautiful eyes gone narrow and smoky with desire. "Wouldn't that be too scandalous?"

Moments later, the sheets and blankets that had looked so pristine were rumpled by the writhing of their bodies. They spent several voluptuous hours there, thoroughly satisfying each other. How nice it would be to have another child with him, Molly thought, for the first time feeling secure enough to consider the notion. But they had plenty of time. She was only twenty-four, Sean-Michel just eight months old—a beautiful, loving little boy who looked just like Raoul though he had her eyes.

For the time being, Sean-Michel deserves our undivided attention, Molly thought. Besides, it might seem a bit unorthodox if we had another child, yet still didn't live under the same roof. With each day that passed, she knew how wise she'd been not to move into the big house where they were enjoying a few stolen moments together. Yet she still didn't feel she could ask the Comte de Montfort to step down to her cozy, less exalted establishment.

Dusk was gathering, and Gabrielle and Marie-Claude were expected back at any time. Molly dressed hastily, kissing her husband goodbye as she slipped out the door.

At the dinner table with his mother and sister that night, Raoul was still glowing with satisfaction and lost in thought. Inevitably his marked inattentiveness caught Gabrielle's notice. Setting his reverie aside, he managed to field her questions about how the day had gone with an admirably bored look.

It wasn't until Molly had returned to her own house that she remembered leaving her earrings on Raoul's dresser. I needn't bother about them tonight, she thought. To do so would just attract attention. Besides, I'll have an opportunity to retrieve them tomorrow. Increasingly friendly despite Molly's unwavering independence, Gabrielle had asked her to dinner. Raoul wouldn't notice her forgotten jewelry. She'd simply arrive a little early and make an excuse to go upstairs.

Just as Molly expected, the earrings were exactly where she'd left them when she returned the following afternoon. As she picked them up, she saw to her surprise that the connecting door to Siobhan's former suite was standing open. Raoul wasn't home from his duties at the National Assembly yet and, drawn like a moth to a flame, Molly entered her late sister's boudoir. An album bound in white leather—the same one Molly had been looking at on her wedding night—was lying open on the bed.

He'd been looking at the pictures of his wedding to Siobhan! Just the thought of the emotions he must have been harboring as he turned the pages twisted like a knife in her abdomen. Her heart aching, she sank down on the coverlet. The album had been left open to a full portrait of the wedding party. A sparklingly lovely Siobhan, a much younger and obviously smitten Raoul, her own skinny, dreamy, childish self stared back at her from the page.

How can he make love to me the way he does if he still cares for Siobhan so much? she asked herself in anguish. How can he care for Siobhan even though she died on her way to a rendezvous with another man? Yet though in all likelihood she'd leave him never to return if Raoul took another woman to bed, Molly knew she'd continue to care for him.

On impulse, she got to her feet and opened the double armoire where most of Siobhan's things were still kept because no one had known how to dispose of them. Yes, there was the soft leather shoulder bag her sister had been carrying when she was killed. Gingerly Molly opened the purse for the first time.

She didn't know what she was seeking—perhaps some clue to Siobhan's hold on the man she loved. At first she didn't find anything unexpected, just a plane ticket, a hairbrush, a makeup case, cigarettes and a mother-of-pearl lighter. Then her hand closed over a plastic compact, the cheap-looking sort of thing her sister would never have used. Her mind went blank with astonishment when she opened it. Siobhan, who had pressured her into surrogate motherhood because she supposedly couldn't have a child, had been taking birth-control pills. Apparently she hadn't wanted to lose her figure. Or disrupt her affair with her lover by having Raoul's baby.

Molly's head spun, and she closed her eyes for a moment. Had Raoul known the truth, tried to warn Molly away, then given in to Siobhan's outrageous plan just as he'd agreed to follow his mother's orders the night he and Molly were wed?

The question festered in her mind throughout dinner with the de Montforts, and she said very little as she picked at the excellent meal. Her silence prompted Raoul and Theo, who was also a guest that evening, to ask if she was ill.

When it was time to leave, Molly's husband offered to walk her home through the garden, and she decided to accept. As he talked about his work, she said nothing. Her mind was running in circles, busily searching for some way to confront him about her discovery.

All such thoughts vanished when she lifted Sean-Michel from his crib and kissed the nape of his neck.

"Sweetheart!" she gasped, searching the child's eyes, which were so like her own. "You're burning up with fever!"

While she ground up baby aspirin and mixed it with orange juice, Raoul was on the phone to the doctor. A family friend who specialized in pediatrics, the elderly physician made an exception despite the lateness of the hour and came over immediately. After he gave Sean-Michel a thorough examination, his verdict was that the baby had some sort of virus.

"It's important you keep him cool—and keep an eye on him," he told the worried parents. "If I'm not mistaken, Raoul was prone to convulsions if his fever went too high when he was a baby. I don't expect him to stop breathing. But if he does, shock his body with successive warm and cold water plunges. That should get him started again."

"Don't you think he should be in the hospital?" Molly asked nervously.

"For tonight, he's probably better off here, with loving parents who will watch him every minute," the doctor said. "In the morning...if his fever doesn't come down...then I'd consider it. We can medicate him intravenously in a hospital setting."

Once the doctor had gone, Molly turned to Raoul. Without even thinking about her discovery of the afternoon, she begged him to stay. "Please...spend the night with us," she said.

He shook his head that she would feel the need to ask. "Wild horses couldn't drag me away...you should know that," he answered.

That night, the two of them slept in shifts as they cared for their sick child with the help of his worried and distraught nurse. His eyes were unnaturally bright, his cheeks flushed with fever. Shortly after 5:00 a.m., Sean-Michel had a convulsive episode. Determined nothing should happen to his son if he could help it, Raoul made a decision.

"Wrap him up in as many blankets as you can," he told Molly. "We're taking him to the hospital."

Chapter Nine

For Molly, the ride to the hospital in Raoul's Citroën
while she clutched Sean-Michel in her arms was a fear-
filled nightmare. If anything happened to him, she wasn't
sure she could go on living. Not Raoul, not all the love in
the world, could compensate.

"Don't worry...he'll be all right." As if he could read
her mind, Raoul squeezed her hand in a clumsy attempt
to comfort her. "The tendency to convulse doesn't mean
there's something seriously wrong with him," he said. "I
did it, too, as a child, apparently. And I'm still here."

Molly tried to smile in return. The look on her husband's face told her he was as worried as she was. Yet she
was more thankful than she'd ever been in her life just to
have him beside her, taking charge of the situation and
caring about Sean-Michel as much as she did. What
would I do without him? she wondered. Come apart at
the seams?

"Our precious baby..." she whispered, kissing their son's hot forehead. "We can't afford to lose him!"

A muscle tightened beside Raoul's mouth. That's what love does, he thought. It makes you hostage. Yet he'd lived most of his life without it and he knew it was more than worth the pain. I'd give my life now for that little boy and consider it well spent, he realized. So would Molly. That's the kind of mother she is.

Moments later they were arriving at the hospital's emergency entrance. Examining Sean-Michel, who had begun to cry fitfully, the physician on duty assured them they'd been right to bring their son in for treatment. The baby would be assigned to a children's intensive care unit upstairs.

"Sean-Michel's temperature is approaching 105 degrees," the doctor admitted when Raoul insisted to know what was happening. "That's not as threatening for a baby as it would be for an adult. But it demands our attention. We've set up an IV and we'll pack him in ice until the fever abates. One of the nurses has already given Dr. Romain a call."

"Will we...be allowed to stay with him?" Molly asked. She was on the verge of tears as her baby was wheeled away by a nurse.

The rather brusque physician softened a little. "Once we get him settled, you and your husband may spend as much time as you like with him, Madame," he said. "We have found children improve more rapidly if their parents remain close at hand."

Sean-Michel looked terribly small and sick when she and Raoul were finally admitted to the cubicle that contained his crib. Molly rested her hand on the metal railing in anguish and frustration. She wanted to *do* something. For the time being, however, everything her baby needed would be provided by others. Her breasts ached with the nourishment he was too ill to accept.

Her tears finally spilling, she turned to Raoul. "I'm terrified," she confessed. "Being here in the hospital is like a bad dream revisited."

In response, he simply opened his arms. Holding her close, he stroked her hair and whispered encouragement. Like her, he remembered all too well the morning Siobhan had died. But he simply couldn't believe fate would take their little boy away from them.

What I said the first night Molly and I made love in her bed was true, he thought. *I feel like a family man. Over these past months, she, I and Sean-Michel have become a family unit whether she's willing to accept it or not. Even if she isn't in love with me, I won't let her send me away at dawn again.*

Gradually the calming effect of having Raoul's arms around her helped Molly regain her courage. Sean-Michel would get better. They had done the right thing.

"Thanks...I'll be okay now," she said, stepping back and dabbing at her eyes with a tissue. "But I could use a cup of coffee. Could you go downstairs and get me one while I keep an eye on the baby?"

All through the long, gray morning and an equally dismal afternoon, she and Raoul drew together as they worried and watched over their child. At times it seemed he was getting a little better. Then his fever would go up again.

With very little sleep to draw on, they'd both reached a state of near-exhaustion when suddenly the fever broke. So glazed looking only a few minutes before, Sean-Michel's eyes were bright and lively once more.

"Ga!" he cried in his unintelligible baby talk as he reached for his mother.

So stalwart throughout the crisis, Raoul felt as if *he* wanted to weep when Molly took the baby in her arms.

"He's not completely over his illness but I feel sure the worst has passed," Dr. Romain told them a few minutes later as he stopped by to check on his young patient. "Everything possible is being done to guard against a relapse. You two should go home and get some rest. The last thing Sean-Michel needs right now is sick parents."

Reluctant to leave yet breathing a mutual sigh of relief, they drove back to Molly's house.

"Believe it or not, I'm *hungry*," she said as they walked inside, retracing the hurried steps they'd taken in such distress many hours before. "Why don't I have Mathilde fix us something to eat?"

Between them, they consumed a huge mushroom and cheese omelet while seated at the butcher-block table in Molly's Provincial, tiled kitchen. Raoul hadn't eaten so informally and with such relish since he was a boy. Savoring every bite, he took it for granted that they'd both get the sleep they needed in Molly's bed.

It was what she expected, too. Though the events that had preceded Sean-Michel's illness—finding the album lying open and Siobhan's birth-control pills—had begun to surface again, they were balanced by Raoul's devotion to their son and his protectiveness of her. Maybe I should settle for what he's able to give, she thought. To me, even the leftover crumbs of his affection are worth more than a banquet with somebody else.

When finally he'd eaten his fill, Raoul called his mother from the pantry phone to assure her the baby was all right. Expressing her relief, Gabrielle didn't ask where he was calling from. He realized she probably guessed. Get used to it, Maman...

It's the wave of the future, he told her silently as he said goodbye.

Following a final cup of coffee, they went upstairs. A bit self-consciously, because they were a tired married couple thinking of sleep, not lovers anticipating a rendezvous, they took off their things. Molly went to the trouble of putting on a nightgown. It made her look very demure.

Yet when she got into bed and Raoul took her in his arms, it seemed the most natural thing in the world.

"Sleep well, *p'tite*," he whispered, planting a kiss on her neck. "I'll be here to make love to you when you wake."

A few days later, Sean-Michel came home from the hospital. He quickly appeared robust again. As if his illness had served as a kind of watershed, banishing their routine of the past, Raoul all but moved into Molly's house. She smiled to see his robe, casual clothes and several suits hanging beside her things in the built-in cupboards of her dressing room. At least three shelves were given over to his underclothes, exquisitely laundered shirts and the shoes her handyman/gardener had begun to polish for him.

We're a de facto family, she thought, getting a warm glow in the vicinity of her heart. Though none of the underlying issues that had once separated them were resolved, it felt just right, waking up with Raoul beside her, chatting with him while he shaved and reading the morning paper in his company.

Unfortunately the news touted in the daily headlines wasn't good. Several French citizens, including a woman and her young daughter, had been snatched by terrorists. According to anonymous sources, the group that had engineered the kidnapping was the same one that had caused Siobhan's death.

Two days later, the terrorists in question claimed responsibility. In a taped interview on Radio Cairo, their spokesman demanded an exchange for his jailed leader.

Very quickly, Raoul found himself in the middle of a government crisis. Though he was sympathetic with the victims and their families, even going so far as to imagine his wife and son in their place, he gave several speeches decrying the willingness of some government officials to deal with terrorists. As a result, he was much in demand by the news media for interviews.

Working long hours and unavoidably absorbed by the hostage dilemma, he didn't want to take his new domestic situation for granted. Though she'd rarely had time for him, Siobhan had always complained bitterly about him being a workaholic. Determined not to alienate Molly in similar fashion, he came home one afternoon with an unexpected proposal.

"What would you say to going away with me to the Loire for a long weekend—just you, me and the baby?" he asked. "I think we need a little time to ourselves."

Molly's heart leaped at the suggestion. Both times they'd been at the fairy-tale château with its long *allée* of venerable trees, storybook turrets and calm river meadows, there had been a crowd of people about. How delightful it would be, she thought, to get away from the political tensions of the capital for a few days—have the château and Raoul all to herself. She decided to give Annie Glynn a holiday.

Though it was already October, the weather continued sunny and mild. They went down on a Friday afternoon in the car, giving Molly her first leisurely glimpse of the French countryside. As they neared Orleans, where yellow leaves trembled on the poplars that edged the road, she began to feel herself unwind. The farther south they got, it seemed, the bluer and more cloudless the sky. The autumn colors were splendid, the breeze soft, the air luminous. The forest of Blois, where they stopped to stretch their legs, was a veritable bonfire of russet and gold.

Jean-Jacques, a family retainer of the de Montforts for years, greeted them at the crested iron gate.

"Bonsoir, M le Comte, Mme la Comtesse," he said, smiling his toothless grin at Sean-Michel. *"Comment va le petit vicomte? Il est presque déjà un homme, je crois!"*

She and Raoul began to agree with the old man that their son was "nearly a man" the following afternoon. Warning the chief gardener to keep workmen away so they wouldn't be disturbed, they'd taken a picnic hamper down to a secluded section of the riverbank. There, they'd spread a soft old blanket beside a century-old planting of willows.

As Molly got out the wine, cheese, crusty bread, grapes and juicy Reinette pears she'd chosen from the kitchen larder, Raoul was tickling their delighted son by burying his face against the child's stomach. She didn't notice when he set the boy upright, holding only his chubby little hands so that Sean-Michel instinctively balanced himself with several baby steps.

The two of them had played that game many times. It always ended with Sean-Michel losing his battle with gravity and landing on his well-padded bottom. When she glanced up this time, however, their son looked as if he might mean business. At ten-and-a-half months and an active crawler, he'd been finding that means of locomotion much too slow for all the exploring he had in mind.

"Call him," Raoul urged. "See if he'll come to you."

Holding out her arms, Molly softly coaxed her beloved child. An intent gleam in his big brown eyes, Sean-Michel considered the invitation. Can I make it on these unsteady legs? he seemed to be asking himself. A space of several feet separated him from the safe haven of his mother's arms.

Suddenly he let go, a fierce look of concentration on his face. Taking one halting step and then another, he grabbed for Molly's outstretched fingers and made it. As his proud parents laughed, he crowed with delight, inordinately pleased with himself.

After lunch and a few more exhibitions of his prowess, Sean-Michel settled down for his afternoon nap. The scene on the riverbank grew still, punctuated only by the calls of birds and the lapping of water. Stretched out on the blanket beside Raoul, Molly had her head against his shoulder.

"I want to make love to you," he said.

She turned a little so that she could see his face. "Here?" she asked. "Won't somebody see us?"

His voice had a husky quality. "I don't think it's likely. We're hidden from view. I warned the workmen away with this very idea in mind."

Feeling a bit brazen and loving it because he was her partner in crime, Molly let Raoul unfasten her blouse and kiss her breasts.

"We don't have to undress completely, you know," he advised, slipping one adventuring hand under her skirt. "But these panties of yours are definitely in the way."

"So's your zipper," she said.

The offending obstacles removed, he covered her atop the blanket. Sean-Michel slept, perhaps dreaming of the future triumphs his newly acquired skill would bring. She moaned at the exquisite pleasure his lovemaking brought. He'd opened his shirt and, as he began to move, her bare breasts brushed his chest.

Though by now they'd made love many times, each coupling was new and different, a just-composed rhapsody of demand and fulfillment. Even so, that time was special. Sensing some kind of barrier had fallen, Raoul went nearly mad with the splendor of it. A shattering climax took them, almost at the same moment.

After they quieted, he rearranged Molly's skirt to cover her thighs. How precious she was to him, he thought. How irreplaceable. If he dared to care for her too much, would she retreat from him? Even now, was he taking advantage of her?

She'd pulled her blouse together without buttoning it and, from his vantage point, he could still see the lush curve of her bosom.

Gently he nudged her bodice aside and kissed her breast. She smiled at him. A moment later she closed her eyes as if in sleep. What would it take to make him love me? she thought. There isn't a part of me he doesn't have now. Yet his affection remains as elusive as before.

She didn't take him to task by look or gesture. The only time he caught a glimpse of sadness in her eyes during their visit was when he accompanied her to her sister's grave. With Raoul at her side, Molly gazed down at Siobhan's simple granite headstone. As much joy as her older sibling had bequeathed her, she hadn't wanted her sister's death.

She laid a bouquet of wildflowers against the stone's base. You didn't really love Raoul or choose to give him the child he wanted, Molly said silently. I do and I have. I'm here now, with him. I only hope someday he'll love me half as much as he loved you.

* * *

When they returned to Paris, the pressure being put on the French government by the terrorist group increased. If a trade was not forthcoming, the international criminals threatened, they'd kill one of their hostages. Raoul was called on to make a response, and French television quickly arranged to cover it. There would be a sizable press contingent from other countries, too.

Escorted by Theo, Molly went to the National Assembly to hear him speak.

"I don't like it that he's become the focus of this thing," she confessed to her friend as they parked in a privileged spot. "That group will do anything to achieve its ends. And it's already killed one member of my family. I'm afraid Raoul could be in some danger."

Theo listened with a frown. "I don't like to say it," he admitted, "but you could be right. After he's finished his speech, I'll have a word with him."

Seated beside Theo in the gallery, Molly looked nervously about, as if she half expected a gang of swarthy men to burst into the room with submachine guns. Don't be silly, she told herself. You're letting your imagination take control.

Her attention was riveted on Raoul when he began his speech. There was no other word for it but impassioned.

Even though he knew it would stir up bad memories for him and his wife, Raoul drew on the sympathy that had been accorded him as a result of Siobhan's death.

"I don't want those people to die, just as I didn't want my first wife to die," he concluded in a ringing voice. "But granting concessions to terrorists is a losing battle. If we concede this time, we may get our people back. Or we may not. Whatever the case, the leader and his henchmen will be free to foment more death and destruction in our airports and other public places. More innocent bystanders will be killed, more French tourists snatched from street corners and subjected to the trauma and indignity of false imprisonment.''

He paused, then continued. ''Yes...I know. If the leader commits another act of terror, we can jail him again...if we can catch him. In that case, his followers will only abduct fresh innocents to trade for his release. The bystanders of this world are like money in the bank to these terrorists. With such infinite 'wealth' at their fingertips, the terror will never end.''

A storm of applause broke out, punctuated by a few jeers. Molly was so proud of her husband that it hurt. Yet even as she pushed her way through the crowd to congratulate him, she felt her fears returning. He's made a target of himself, she thought.

During the press conference that had been scheduled after his speech, someone slipped Raoul a note. Opening it he read the threat it contained directly into the microphones. The terrorists had vowed to get him for his opposition to their demands.

'' 'We're curious to learn, M le Député, whether your courage extends to your own person. Never doubt it—you'll be hearing from us.' ''

Immediately following the press conference, a twenty-four-hour guard was arranged for Raoul, Molly, Sean-Michel and Raoul's family by the *Sûreté*. Lying in her bed with Raoul that night, Molly felt as if they were huddled together in the heart of a fortress. She was terribly afraid for her husband's safety.

''You must promise me you'll be *very* careful,'' she whispered as they said good-night. ''Sean-Michel and I can't afford to lose you.''

Touched at her concern, Raoul drew her closer in his arms. ''Nothing in this world could keep me from you and our son, *mon p'tit chou*," he told her. "And that's a promise I plan to keep."

The following morning, trailed by her *Sûreté* guard, Molly drove to the shop, leaving Sean-Michel in the care of Annie, Mathilde, the handyman and the taciturn policeman who had been charged with his welfare. She hadn't wanted to go.

Raoul had insisted. Overriding her objections, he'd gone to his office as usual, stating he wouldn't allow anyone to disrupt their lives. The guard assigned to him would stand by the door and shoot terrorists dead as they entered, he'd assured her jokingly. Molly hadn't found it funny in the least.

In no mood to deal with the demands of customers, she left that task to Mimi and a second woman she'd hired when business had exceeded her expectations. Closeting herself in her office, she tried to concentrate on ordering the next season's line of clothing.

Before long, there was a tap at the door. Mimi poked her head inside. "*Pardon,* Molly," she said. "But the guard from the *Sûreté* went across the street to get something to eat. Just after he left, this man in a chauffeur's uniform came in, asking for you. He says he's assigned to your husband at the National Assembly, that he must speak with you."

Hesitating a moment, Molly allowed the man to come in. Her *Sûreté* guard would be back in a moment, after all. And besides, the terrorists' threat had been aimed at Raoul.

Dressed in an impeccable gray uniform and cap, the chauffeur had a deferential manner. He showed her his credentials before she could speak. He seemed to be some sort of policeman.

"What do you want?" Molly asked.

"I'm sorry to inform you, madame, that your son may be in some danger," he said. "Your husband has asked me to take you directly home."

Sean-Michel in danger? Molly's heart skipped a beat. "What happened?" she cried, fear gripping her like a vise.

Her visitor appeared to hesitate. "I'm not certain," he admitted. "I only have my orders."

Why hadn't Raoul called her himself? Molly wondered. But perhaps he'd tried and gotten a busy signal. She reached for the phone.

The chauffeur-policeman's gloved hand closed over hers. "Better not," he advised. "Your husband specifically asked that you not telephone, as the lines may be tapped."

Even as they spoke, Molly's fear for Sean-Michel was mounting. Her *Sûreté* man was just across the street. Should she wait until he returned? Or leave without him?

"Please, madame," the officer who was dressed as a chauffeur begged. "We must be quick."

Molly hovered in a quandary, afraid of making the wrong move. The man's credentials seemed in order. Every second she delayed might be that much worse for Sean-Michel.

Overcome by a mother's fears, she decided to cooperate. Without a word to Mimi, who was in the midst of a sale, she walked out of the shop. Her companion guided her lightly by the arm.

It was only when she got into the waiting limousine and found herself sandwiched in between two men holding automatic pistols that she realized what a terrible mistake she'd made. In her furor to protect her son, she'd exposed him to the potential heartbreak of losing his mother. Meanwhile, Raoul would be subjected to a severe test of his resolve not to let terrorists blackmail the French government.

What a fool I've been! she castigated herself, daring to struggle with her captors. A moment later, something heavy came crashing down on the back of her skull.

Chapter Ten

Raoul was just leaving his office for the assembly floor when his secretary told him he had an urgent call. "The man won't give his name," she said in agitation. "But I think you'd better talk to him."

A worried frown creased his forehead. Jeanne was scarcely an alarmist. If she didn't like the sound of his caller, then he didn't, either. "Tell M Raynaud I'll be with him in a moment," he said, picking up the phone and uttering a brusque, *"Allô."*

"I saw you read our note on television, M le Député," a man said in a husky voice.

A glowing red light on the phone panel announced that the call had come in on Raoul's private line. He rarely gave out the number to anyone. Somehow they'd managed to get hold of it. The simple fact didn't bode well.

"I received a threat from some cowardly sewer rat who was too afraid to show his face, if that's what you mean," he answered, screening the worry from his voice.

"It's happened before. What do you want? I've got work to do."

"In your speech yesterday, you made some very strong statements," his caller replied. "You advised the government not to deal with us . . . even if the lives of innocent people were at stake. Or should I say the lives of innocent *strangers*?"

Raoul's sense of foreboding increased with every word.

"We've decided to give you a lesson in reality, M le Député," the man continued. "What would you say to a slightly different equation? Freedom for our compatriot in exchange for the life of one dear to you?"

Before Raoul could demand an explanation, the line went dead. Propelled by fear, he quickly punched out the number of Molly's shop, then called her house. Both lines were busy. The maid, Martine, answered at his mother's residence. Neither she nor Gabrielle knew anything.

Surely the caller was a crank, someone who disapproved of the stand he'd taken and had decided to make him sweat a little. But he didn't believe it. The undertone of anger and cruelty in the man's voice had been frighteningly real.

With no further thought of joining his colleague on the assembly floor, Raoul ran out of the building and got into the Citroën. He was frantic. Should he run by the shop? Or drive to the house first? The shop was closer. Nearly stripping the car's gears in his haste, he roared out of the parking lot as his security guard raced to keep up with him.

A tearful, apologetic Mimi and a humiliated *Sûreté* officer greeted him at *Rosie O'Meara's-Paris*. His sense of something terrible having happened only increased.

"Where's my wife?" he demanded, glancing from one unhappy face to the other. "I want to talk to her...*now*!"

Wringing her hands, Mimi described the circumstances of Molly's departure. "You didn't follow them?" Raoul asked incredulously, grabbing the policeman by his lapels.

Shamefaced and clearly filled with self-loathing thanks to his dereliction of duty, the man didn't call him on it. "They disabled my car," he admitted. "But I got their license number. By now, all of Paris will be looking for them."

What good would that do? Thrusting the policeman aside, Raoul tore out the door and flung himself into his car. If they lay a finger on Molly, I'll kill the lot of them, he vowed as he streaked across the Seine to the Rue Pierre. I don't care if they try me for murder.

Yet if anything happened to Molly, he realized, Sean-Michel would need him more than ever.

To Raoul's intense relief, the baby was happily playing in his nursery guarded by Annie and the hulking officer who had been assigned to him. He smiled when he saw his father. "Da-da-da-da-da! A-ga!" he jabbered, holding out his chubby arms.

Scooping up his son, Raoul hugged the child so fiercely he protested and tried to wriggle free. Thank God you're safe, little man, he thought, setting the boy back down among his blocks and plastic fire engines. But they had Molly. And for Raoul, that was like having his heart carved out of his chest.

He walked into her room—*their* room now—and sat down on the bed. Only that morning he'd held her in his arms and tried to quell her fears. If only he'd listened to her! He appreciated the value of feminine intuition now that it was too late.

At least he could take some additional precautions to protect Sean-Michel. Picking up the bedroom phone, he called a private agency and hired more bodyguards. The action brought a small measure of relief. Yet he knew their beloved baby's welfare couldn't console him if anything happened to that baby's mother.

Molly! he thought. Skinny twelve-year-old in an impossibly childish dress, dancing with me under protest at the Northland Country Club. Lovely young woman wearing softest apricot, resting her hand against the wall of a Roman ruin and sensing the passage of centuries. Bride in mourning clothes, sweet lover in nothing but her satin skin.

With a lump in his throat, Raoul saw her clinging to his hand as she pushed their baby out into the world. Nursing Sean-Michel at her breast. Shyly blocking his path in her seductive red evening gown as she dared to bridge their separateness.

How he loved her! If only he could erase the passage of time, lie once more with her on a sun-drenched blanket in the river meadow. He buried his face in his hands.

Theo arrived at almost the same moment as Raoul's sorely tried bodyguard. Mathilde showed them both upstairs.

"M le Comte . . ." the bodyguard began irritably.

Clearly realizing his friend was at the limit of his endurance, Theo shook his head. "Leave us for a moment, if you don't mind," he told the policeman. "I promise . . . he won't go anywhere again without telling you first."

For several minutes, Theo said nothing. He simply sat beside Raoul on the bed with his arm around the latter's shoulders. At last Raoul got control of himself. "I want to *do* something," he insisted in a husky voice. "Anything you can think of that would help."

Together they decided they should go to *Sûreté* headquarters. If there'd been any breaks in the case, the police would be able to fill them in. But there hadn't been any. As they expected, the authorities insisted they were doing everything possible to uncover Molly's whereabouts.

"It would be best, M le Député," reasoned the mustachioed chief inspector, Jacques Gronchet, "if you would return home and await the kidnappers' call. I've already sent a contingent of my men there to set up equipment for recording and tracing it."

Reluctantly Raoul saw the wisdom in his advice. Had they passed the *Sûreté* electronics experts going the other way? he wondered. Or, as was more likely, had the crew gone to the wrong house?

When he explained the dual nature of his residence, Chief Inspector Gronchet didn't raise an eyebrow at its irregularity. "In that case, monsieur," he said, "we shall monitor *both* phones."

As they returned to the Rue Pierre house where he'd found such joy, Raoul began to consider how he would answer the terrorists' almost certain demands. "What am I going to do?" he groaned. "They'll insist on a retraction of my position against trading hostages. And in good conscience I can't offer them one. Besides, I'm just one voice. I don't control the government."

Perhaps wisely, Theo didn't answer.

"The hell of it is," Raoul added after a moment, "I *want* to give in. How can I sacrifice Molly for my principles? I love her too much!"

At that, his friend threw him a sharp look. "Does Molly know how you feel?" he asked. "Have you *told* her so?"

The fact that he hadn't was written all over Raoul's face. "No," he admitted. "I haven't wanted to put any additional pressure on her, given our situation...."

Theo shook his head. "Forgive me, *mon ami*. You're one of the most intelligent men I know. But in this case, you've behaved like a fool."

As if he partly regretted his harsh words, he laid one hand on Raoul's arm. Once they'd returned to Molly's small but elegant abode, he hung around while Raoul played pensively with his son and waited for the kidnappers to call.

Molly dug her way out of the stupor into which her captors had plunged her with all the determination and difficulty of a blind person climbing out of a well. Her head hurt. It was throbbing as if someone had bashed it with a hammer. Dreams of mayhem and peril, hideous dreams in which she struggled to protect Sean-Michel, kept trying to pull her back into the void.

At last she opened her eyes. She was dizzy. Weak as if from a long illness. And mercifully alone. Gingerly her fingers explored the massive knot on the back of her head. Moments after she'd gotten into the limousine, she guessed, one of the men had hit her over the head with the butt of his pistol.

To her surprise, she wasn't tied up or blindfolded. She seemed to be lying on a narrow bed in a starkly furnished bedroom very unlike her own. She got the feeling it was situated on the second floor of an ancient, poorly maintained house.

Sitting up and then steadying herself against a blinding flash of pain, she got to her feet. Perhaps she could find some way out of there. But the door was locked. Shutters had been nailed over the grimy, old-fashioned windows. She wasn't sure what part of the city she was in.

Just then a man's voice came over a crude loudspeaker that had been nailed up over the door. "Welcome to our humble abode, Mme de Montfort," he sneered. "You will note we haven't bound and gagged you. If you wish this privilege to continue, don't scream or try to attract attention. When your husband has had sufficient time to reevaluate his position on dealing with us, we'll allow you to speak to him by phone. In the meantime, we invite you to partake of a hot meal, which at this moment is being delivered to you by dumbwaiter."

For the first time, Molly noted a wall panel that indicated the presence of an old-fashioned device for transporting food, laundry and other items between floors. The dumbwaiter creaked to a halt behind it.

Awkwardly sliding back the panel, she withdrew a chipped bowl containing some kind of meatless stew made of lentils and chard. On the battered table beside the bed where she'd regained consciousness a spoon and a carafe of water awaited her. Somewhere in the house someone had turned on a radio.

Was it possible that her seemingly innocent lunch was drugged? Somehow Molly doubted it. If they didn't need to tie her up, they wouldn't need to drug her, either—at least not until it was time to remove her from the house.

Far from hungry but determined to regain her strength, she sat down on the bed and began to eat. To her surprise, the concoction with its hint of garlic and coriander was quite palatable. Now what? she thought, her

energy returning. I've got to find some way to get word
to Raoul. But I don't even know where I am. Or if anything's happened to him and Sean-Michel.

Speculatively her eye lit on the dumbwaiter again. It
was *very* small—too small, her captors apparently believed, to offer her refuge or a way out of the room. But
was it really?

As an experiment, Molly sent the empty bowl back
down by pressing the appropriate button. The device
groaned into action at her bidding. She held her breath,
wondering if anyone was in the kitchen area below to receive it. If so, he or she wouldn't be alone in the house.
The man whose arrogant message had been delivered to
her via loudspeaker would hardly stoop to culinary tasks.

She was curious about a few other things, too. Could
her captors hear the dumbwaiter's movement above the
sound of their music? More importantly, was there a
phone in the kitchen? Would it be possible to see something of her surroundings from one of the downstairs
windows?

The most crucial questions of all were the simplest
ones. Did she have a chance to escape? The courage to
try?

Forcing herself to calm, Molly waited a full half hour
before trying her next experiment. Pressing a second
button, she summoned the dumbwaiter back to her floor.
Yes, the bowl was still there! No one had claimed it. And
the door would slide open from the inside! Now if she
could only fit and find some way to press the send button and scramble inside before the device started back
downstairs.

Removing the bowl, she tried cramming herself into
the tiny space. It was very difficult. But she was quite slim

now and with a little practice she was just able to manage it.

Her heart in her throat, she pressed the Down button and crawled inside. What seemed like an eternity later, she was carefully sliding the panel back in a bleak, disheveled kitchen. There was nobody about.

Her senses sharpened by fear, Molly took quick inventory of her surroundings. Music and male conversation in a foreign language met her ears from what was probably the front of the house. There was no covering over a window that overlooked the alley. She could see a faded sign that advertised international records over one of the service entrances on the opposite side.

She also spotted one of the men who'd been in the car with her. Though he was simply leaning against a wall, smoking a cigarette, she knew he had a gun and had been set to guard the rear entry. If she tried to escape that way, she'd be shot.

All right, then, she thought. Where's the telephone?

As if placed there by the hands of angels, a phone was hanging on the wall of an adjacent pantry that was piled with foodstuffs and what were doubtless cartons of ammunition and explosives. Did she dare pick it up? What if one of her captors was already on the line?

Realizing she must take the chance, Molly lifted the receiver. To her profound relief, a dial tone met her ear. Quickly she entered her home number. If he were able, Raoul would be at the other end of the line, watching over their son and awaiting word of her.

He answered on the second ring. "Molly!" he exclaimed. "Where are you? Are you all right?"

"Listen, don't talk," she whispered. "I don't know exactly where I am. It's a very old house. I can see a sign that says *Disques Mondiales* across the alley. They've been holding me in an upstairs room. I sneaked down to the kitchen to call . . .''

"Are you all right?" Raoul interrupted to ask again. "They haven't hurt you?"

She didn't have time to answer him. Footsteps were slowly advancing in the direction of the kitchen. Hurriedly replacing the receiver, Molly ducked into the dumbwaiter and slid the panel shut.

At the Rue Pierre house, Raoul was beside himself with fear. She was alive! Apparently well! And putting herself into unnecessary danger. What had caused her to terminate their conversation so abruptly? Had she been discovered? And made to pay a price?

"Did you trace the call?" he demanded feverishly of the police technicians who had set up their equipment in an adjoining room.

There was a moment's hesitation as the chief technician conferred with his subordinate. "We don't have the specific number, monsieur," he admitted. "But we've narrowed the call to a particular area of Paris . . . Belleville-Menilmontant."

Seconds later, the phone shrilled again. This time it was the chief inspector. "We listened in on your wife's call," he told Raoul without preamble. "One of my men thinks he knows the location, thanks to Mme de Montfort's mention of the record store. Commandos are moving into the area as we speak."

"I want to be there!"

Refusing to listen when the police inspector urged caution, Raoul entrusted Sean-Michel to his nurse and bodyguards and rushed out the door. Theo offered to drive, fearing he'd get in an accident. Raoul's security guard barely managed to pile into the back seat.

They arrived in the working-class, ethnic bastion of eastern Paris as government commandos were fanning out in the alleyways. Spotting them as they got out of Theo's car, Chief Inspector Gronchet hurried over.

"I know you're worried about your wife, monsieur," he told Raoul earnestly. "But you must stand back. It won't solve anything if you manage to get yourself shot."

Trapped in the dumbwaiter by the presence of several terrorists in the kitchen, Molly didn't dare move. If they went upstairs, they'd find her missing and begin to search for her. Ultimately they'd find her. Maybe even kill her for disobeying them.

If I get through this alive, she thought, I'm going to tell Raoul how much I love him. It won't matter if he doesn't feel the same way. Life's too short, too fragile for us to keep secrets from each other.

As Raoul and Theo watched and waited, there was an eerie silence in the surrounding streets. Police had warned traffic and pedestrians away from the area. Raoul supposed they'd unobtrusively emptied the shops that surrounded their target, as well. Would the terrorists who were holding Molly begin to sense something was wrong and harm her in consequence? Before the police could flush them from their hiding place, would they spirit her away?

If and when I get her back safe, I'm never going to let her go again, Raoul vowed. Never mind that ours was a marriage of convenience. Or that she might have chosen differently if it hadn't been for Sean-Michel. When we're together, the fifteen years' difference between us doesn't seem to matter. Neither does the fact that I was once married to Siobhan.

He loved Molly. Maybe he'd always loved her. His feelings for her grew deeper with each day that passed. Theo's right, he thought. I need to tell her. Pride can't be allowed to stand in the way. With the awful clarity afforded by the situation in which they found themselves, he knew his silence had been partly that, not just an admirable reluctance to ask too much in return.

Suddenly a spate of gunfire broke out and he was running toward it despite Chief Inspector Gronchet's warning shouts. He arrived at the scene in time to see several terrorists being led away in handcuffs. Identifying himself to one of the commandos, he was allowed to enter. There was no sign of Molly anywhere.

"M de Montfort?" the commando leader called to him from a front room that had obviously been used by the terrorists as their staging area. Street maps of Paris, shortwave radio equipment and a cache of weapons were jumbled on a large table.

Quickly Raoul joined the rangy officer who, like his men, was wearing camouflage. "Where's my *wife*?" he asked, terrified Molly might lie bleeding somewhere.

The man gave him a worried look. "We've searched the house and we're certain we've arrested everyone," he said. "If she's hiding, she might not realize that. But she'd recognize your voice. Would you mind calling out her name?"

Huddled inside the dumbwaiter and almost paralyzed with fear from all the gunfire, Molly heard Raoul shouting for her. "Here!" she screamed. "I'm in here!"

Like a madman, he rushed into the kitchen and looked frantically about. He didn't see the dumbwaiter panel right away. Then he spotted it and pulled it open with all his strength. The stiffness of her limbs notwithstanding, Molly crawled out and flung herself into his arms.

For a moment there in the shabby, unfamiliar kitchen, time stood still. "Is Sean-Michel safe?" Molly asked, setting it in motion again.

"He's fine." Letting himself shake a little, Raoul crushed her to him. "Driving Annie and his bodyguards crazy, I expect."

Molly gave a heartfelt sigh. She could feel the tension flowing out of her body. "I love you so much, Raoul," she whispered. "I decided if I ever got out of that dumbwaiter alive, I was going to tell you so."

His preconceived notions about how she felt went into a tailspin. Molly loved him! Could she possibly mean it? He'd been willing, more than willing, to settle for so much less.

His voice was rough with emotion as he answered her. "You don't have to say that."

"I know I don't." Tears of release ran down Molly's cheeks. He hadn't responded in kind. Yet she was happier than she'd ever dreamed possible. She felt as if a stone had been lifted from her heart. "You didn't guess?" she added. "Ever since I was twelve..."

The thought of the gangly, impressionable girl she'd once been developing a crush on him—one that had blossomed into the love of a woman—was almost more than Raoul could bear. With a groan he kissed her mouth, her nose, her eyelids.

"Ah, Molly," he murmured. "I love you, too, sweetheart . . . so much that this arrangement of ours has been like a thorn in my flesh. I want to be your husband in every way possible, to cherish you forever. We have a lot of talking to do."

There'd be time for it now. They had the rest of their lives together. Fresh tears of happiness shone in Molly's eyes.

Smiling as if he'd overheard part of their conversation, the commando leader approached. "If you don't mind, M le Comte," he said, "it might be a good idea to take your wife home. We still have a lot of evidence to sift through."

Tamely apologizing for interfering with his work, Raoul thanked the officer and walked Molly to the car. After a word with Chief Inspector Gronchet, they headed home with Raoul's arms wrapped about Molly in the back seat and Theo behind the wheel. Despite all that had happened and the bump on her head that still throbbed intermittently, she had only one thought. Raoul loved her! She felt like the luckiest woman in the world.

The moment they arrived, Molly insisted on running upstairs to throw her arms around Sean-Michel. Sweet baby, she thought, kissing his rosy cheeks. Your mommy's so glad to be home. And so *very* grateful you're all right.

A few minutes later, Dr. Romain arrived. Summoned by Raoul, he checked the bump on Molly's head, shined a light in her eyes and diagnosed a mild concussion. "She'll be fine," he told them, "with a little rest."

It didn't seem as if any would be immediately forthcoming. Following the doctor's visit, Molly took a call from the United States. Matt and Aunt Rosie had heard about her abduction on the news and they were terribly worried. Jubilant that she'd been rescued, her brother admitted he still felt some concern.

"Don't," Molly told him. "No lesser person than the chief inspector of the *Sûreté* has assured us that the terrorist who masterminded my kidnapping was among those captured by his men. He won't be giving us any more trouble for a long, long time."

Her face shining with relief, Annie drew Molly a warm bath. Before immersing herself in it, Molly stopped to talk with her mother-in-law, who had hurried across the garden at the news that she was safe. To Raoul's amazement, the two women embraced. It seemed a whole new era was beginning.

Fixing his wife a brandy, Raoul realized Molly had a certain amount of nervous energy to work off, not to mention the need for some coddling and a thorough rest before he showed her in a tangible way just how much he loved her. Scooping up their son and balancing the balloon-shaped brandy glass in his other hand, he joined her in the *salle de bain*.

Sipping at her brandy and luxuriating in billows of scented suds, Molly gazed into the tawny eyes of the man she loved. Her nightmare was over. The best part of her life was just beginning.

"There are a few things I'd like to clear up," Raoul said, allowing Sean-Michel a handful of bubbles to play with. "Number one on my list is your misconception that I made love to you on our wedding night at my mother's request."

Molly digested the revelation. "So Marie-Claude was lying. Why didn't you tell me?"

"Actually, she wasn't," he admitted. "Maman *did* demand that I consummate our marriage to keep you from getting an annulment. I refused."

"But then... I don't understand."

He bent to kiss her neck. "It was the sweet temptation of holding you in my arms when I found you crying over that album that broke down my resistance."

"Yet you let me think..."

"I felt I'd be taking even greater advantage of your generosity if I made a clean breast of things and asked you to stay. Anyway, I expected you to tell me *no*."

Molly stared at him in disbelief. How could such a marvelous man be so misguided? "You're too much!" she accused, her mouth curving as she threw a handful of soap suds in his face.

Tenderly drying Molly off, Raoul held out her robe. "Come, my love," he urged. "First let's put our son to bed. Then I'll tuck you in. You need to get some rest."

"Only if you'll join me."

Nestled beneath a down quilt in her husband's arms, Molly felt she was truly home at last. Lovingly he pressured her to sleep a while. But she didn't want to. Safe in his affection and feeling much better after her hot bath and brandy, she wanted to make love instead. She opened her robe beneath the covers.

"No," Raoul protested half-heartedly.

"Yes . . . most *definitely* yes," Molly replied.

That evening, as dusk gathered over Paris, and Annie fed Sean-Michel his supper, Molly soared out of control in her husband's arms. Thanks to the new depth of their relationship and the loving acceptance each of them felt, that lovemaking was their most profound yet. Racked by wave after wave of pleasure, she felt permanently linked to the man she loved, at one with the universe.

Afterward, as they drifted together on a sea of contentment, she dared to ask him about something that was on her mind. "Speaking of the wedding album," she murmured, "I'm curious why you got it out just before Sean-Michel went to the hospital."

Raoul raised one eyebrow in surprise. "How did you know about that?"

"I left my earrings in your room. When I went to reclaim them, the door to Siobhan's old suite was open."

He was silent a moment. "I guess you're wondering why I'd be poring over pictures of your sister if it's you I love."

Phrased that way, her emphasis on the incident seemed petty. "Never mind...it doesn't matter," Molly said.

"Ah, but it does." Tilting her chin with one finger, Raoul looked deeply into her eyes. "I was looking for a picture of *you*, dearest Molly," he said. "You at twelve, in that funny dress you wore...."

Relief coursed through her in a flood. She hadn't realized just how much finding the album had upset her. "That was a very *pretty* dress!" she protested.

Raoul couldn't help smiling at her injured feminine pride. "If you say so," he said. "In my opinion, it's better to let go of ghosts. But I'd like you to understand how I felt about Siobhan. When she and I were married, I was infatuated with her in an immature way. If I loved her at all, it was as a boy loves. *You* Molly, I love with all the manly ardor I possess."

"Oh, Raoul...." Overcome that she should mean so much to him, she buried her face against his shoulder.

"Siobhan and I were wrong for each other from the beginning," he added. "Our marriage was over long before you came to Paris a year and a half ago and realized what was going on. I'd been celibate a long, long time, my darling, when I first took you in my arms."

If only she'd known the truth!

Though she was still undecided about the pros and cons of surrogate motherhood, Molly realized that—in her case, at least—it had turned out for the best. The love that had prompted her to accede to her sister's wishes had been rewarded a thousandfold.

At last she could lay her guilt for loving Siobhan's husband to rest. While her sister had been alive, she'd fiercely battled her unwanted emotions. Now the gift of life to Sean-Michel and Raoul's need for her had canceled out her debt.

Daring to forgive herself, Molly decided not to tell him about Siobhan's birth-control pills. She let past hurts and deceptions scatter like dry leaves in a windstorm as Raoul's mouth claimed hers and they made love to each other again.

*   *   *   *   *

WRITTEN IN THE STARS

MAN FROM THE NORTH COUNTRY
by Laurie Paige

What does Cupid have planned for
the Aquarius man? Find out in February in
MAN FROM THE NORTH COUNTRY by
Laurie Paige—the second book in our
WRITTEN IN THE STARS series!

Brittney Chapel tried explaining the sensible
side of marriage to confirmed bachelor
Daniel Montclair, but the gorgeous grizzly bear
of a man from the north country wouldn't
respond to reason. What was a woman to do
with an unruly Aquarian? Tame him!

Spend the most romantic month of the year with
MAN FROM THE NORTH COUNTRY by
Laurie Paige in February... only from
Silhouette Romance.

Silhouette Special Edition

proudly presents
the long-awaited "prequel" volume of

★ LOVE AND GLORY ★

by
LINDSAY McKENNA
Dawn of Valor

In the summer of '89, Silhouette Special Edition premiered three novels celebrating America's men and women in uniform: LOVE AND GLORY, by bestselling author Lindsay McKenna. Featured were the proud Trayherns, a military family as bold and patriotic as the American flag—three siblings valiantly battling the threat of dishonor, determined to triumph . . . in love and glory.

Now, discover the roots of the Trayhern brand of courage, as parents Chase and Rachel relive their earliest heartstopping experiences of survival and indomitable love, in

Dawn of Valor, Silhouette Special Edition #649

This month, experience the thrill of LOVE AND GLORY—from the very beginning!

Available at your favorite retail outlet, or order your copy by sending your name, address, zip or postal code, along with a check or money order (please do not send cash) for $2.95, plus 75¢ postage and handling, payable to Silhouette Reader Service to:

In the U.S.
3010 Walden Ave.
P.O. Box 1396
Buffalo, NY 14269-1396

In Canada
P.O. Box 609
Fort Erie, Ontario
L2A 5X3

Please specify book title with your order. Canadian residents add applicable federal and provincial taxes.

Silhouette Books®

DV-1A

Take 4 bestselling love stories FREE

Plus get a FREE surprise gift!

SILHOUETTE·INTIMATE·MOMENTS®

FEBRUARY FROLICS!

This February, we've got a special treat in store for you: four terrific books written by four brand-new authors! From sunny California to North Dakota's frozen plains, they'll whisk you away to a world of romance and adventure.

Look for

L.A. HEAT (IM #369) by Rebecca Daniels
AN OFFICER AND A GENTLEMAN (IM #370) by Rachel Lee
HUNTER'S WAY (IM #371) by Justine Davis
DANGEROUS BARGAIN (IM #372) by Kathryn Stewart

They're all part of February Frolics, coming to you from Silhouette Intimate Moments—where life is exciting and dreams do come true.

FF-1

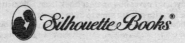 *Silhouette Books*®

SILHOUETTE·INTIMATE·MOMENTS®

NORA ROBERTS
Night Shadow

People all over the city of Urbana were asking, Who was that masked man?

Assistant district attorney Deborah O'Roarke was the first to learn his secret identity . . . and her life would never be the same.

The stories of the lives and loves of the O'Roarke sisters began in January 1991 with NIGHT SHIFT, Silhouette Intimate Moments #365. And if you want to know more about Deborah and the man behind the mask, look for NIGHT SHADOW, Silhouette Intimate Moments #373, available in March at your favorite retail outlet.

NITE-1

 *Silhouette Books®*